UNWITTINGLY IMMORTAL

Carey J. Burke

UNWITTINGLY IMMORTAL

ISBN: 978-0-578-60600-2

Dedicated to
Mary, Borghild, Ron, Dave, Mel, Martie, and Bill

FORWARD

I call this a novel only because no one believes me when I share what I know. They just smile that knowing smile—like I've lost my marbles. I'm not kidding, something wonderful has begun, and there's no stopping it. You can put this book down and turn your back to what's coming, but it won't change anything. Tech will soon bring an end to mortality—and in all honesty, it began with a stereo.

Chapter 1

Daniel Dutton's latest novel, his eighth, was titled *Electric Seance*. He had only the Author's Note to add before the thing was done, before he could forward it to his publisher.

When he was finished, the author's note read: "While this story is fiction, the devices depicted here are within our reach today using existing electronic and electromagnetic technologies."

Later that night, somewhere around 2:00 A.M., the Duttons' stereo turned itself on at full volume. The speakers might as well have been under the bed, the entire house was vibrating to the strains of *Lady Madonna* at an ear-blasting level.

Dan awoke with a start, saying,"What the hell!" He sat up and covered his ears.

Beside him, Sarah turned on the lamp and put her fingers to her ears. Her lips were moving, but he missed what she said. She got close and repeated slowly, "Do you think there's a prowler?"

In the same fashion, Dan said, "You stay here, honey. I'll go check." Sarah nodded. He jumped out of bed and reached into the closet for his old *Louisville Slugger* before leaving the room.

With the bat under his arm, and fingers to his ears, Daniel reached the stair landing, turned on the light with an elbow, and made his way down the stairs to the living room. Again using his elbow, he jabbed at the stereo's power button and uncovered his ears. The silence itself was almost deafening.

With his bat raised, Daniel cautiously inspected the first floor—and found nothing. Returning to the stereo he muttered, "How the…?" and stood there for a long silent moment in thought.

When it came to him, he smiled and dropped the bat.

It was the Author's Note.

Anyone understanding Dan's reasoning would have felt certain he'd gone nuts, out of his mind. Well, anyone but his dad.

The answer was right in front of him. He was looking at it. The stereo was *proof* someone had been looking over his shoulder as he typed the Author's Note. More than that, his secret audience had to have been reading his story all along, and fully understood the implications when Daniel revealed that the tale's basis was much more than fiction. And so, his secret reader had reached for whatever electronic device was at hand, in an effort to make his or her presence known.

This was wonderful! It was beyond anything Dan could have hoped for.

He decided to set up a simple test, a way to prove that the stereo hadn't been a fluke occurrence, that he wasn't imagining a connection that didn't exist.

If it happened again, it would be proof of sorts, enough for a working hypothesis anyway. Dan grinned as he thought about the implications. He reached over and ever-so-slowly and deliberately turned the stereo's volume knob all the way down.

Then, not so coolly, and in a bit of a panic, Dan scoured the entire downstairs for the remote—even in the refrigerator. His proof would never stand if he couldn't isolate the damned thing. When he finally found it, the remote was where it should have been—snug beside the stereo receiver.

Oh, well.

Dan stuffed it into a nearby drawer and went back to bed.

Five hours later, that same blessed morning, Daniel made it back down to the living room and checked the stereo.

It was on again!

He couldn't wait to tell his dad.

Daniel's father, Jason Dutton, was a pathologist and scientist of no small repute, though he differed from his contemporaries in his total lack of professional ego. His single preoccupation was with leaving the world a better place than he'd found it. And like his son, Jason Dutton was a writer—though the senior Dutton's writings were decidedly nonfiction.

There had been a major uproar in the medical, psych, and scientific communities with the publication of his bestseller, *DEAD, BUT NOT GONE: An Open-minded Scientist's Take on Life and Death.*

Never before had a man of science and medicine spoken so unequivocally on such matters. 'That all living things have an overriding spiritual component.' Contrary to what he called 'The Popular Scientific Myth: That living things were no more than organic, self-replicating, self-animating, evolution-driven machines.'

His assertions more than rubbed the defenders of Big Medicine, Big Pharma, and the Scientific Method the wrong way. But it was a subsequent death threat that, in the end, elevated Jason to even higher levels of celebrity and eventually led him to begin speaking on the subject publicly.

It was the ironic brand of coincidence that found Daniel's accidental insight arriving just a few days after his father had been given a decidedly inauspicious diagnosis. The two met that same morning at their favorite coffee shop.

Jason looked well and was every bit as enthusiastic as his son regarding the implications of last night's inadvertent experiment. He took his first sip of coffee and said, "What did Jessy think when it happened?"

"She was away at a friend's pajama party. You know Jessica, she's a very sensitive child and sorry she missed it. She's been saying all along, since we moved in, that our place is haunted. 'An old lady and her cat,' she says. Even knows her name, Marla Culpepper. It's crazy that I haven't already gone down to the courthouse and looked up the deed's history. I will now!"

"I sure love that sweet child," said Jason. "Listen to what she told me the other day—'Only two more weeks and I'll be exactly six-and-a-half.'"

"Yeah, that sounds like Jessica. Six-and-a-half, going on thirty. And she loves you, Dad. You're very special to her."

Jason smiled. "So, tell me more about last night. Do you have any idea how that happened?"

"I do. I think it was the receiver's infrared link to the remote. Of course, the remote itself had nothing to do with it. It was in a drawer when the stereo was turned on the second time."

"So where do we start?" asked Jason. "You're the electronics engineer."

"Well, if the infrared link is the key, I'm thinking I could rig a circuit that our eavesdropper could actually communicate through, even if we had to resort to something like Morse Code. Still, if we wind up going in a totally different direction—this event shows us *it's possible*."

As hopeful as Dan was about last night, his greatest concern was their immediate problem—his father's prognosis. He asked, "Dr. Kravitz did say a year, right?"

"He said six months, maybe as much as a year. Give or take."

"I'll get on this research full-time. Like you've always said, Dad, 'Things happen for a reason.' Your prognosis, and last night, are a classic example. We'll figure it out. I'll make it work, somehow. I have to make it work. I love you, Dad."

"I know you will, Daniel. I love you too."

Later that same week, Jessica and her grandfather were on a nature walk along their favorite stream. "Look at this, Grandpa!" said Jessica. "It's sorta like the piece of limestone you have in your den."

Jason smiled and said, "Let's see, Jessy. Oh, wow! You're right. What a find! Lots of fossils in that one. Okay, what am I going to ask you?"

"I know, Grandpa. It's like when we play *Carnivore or Herbivore*, except these are fossils. So you're gonna ask if they're vertebrates or invertebrates."

"So what's a vertebrate, sweetie?"

"A vertebrate's an animal with a backbone."

"And how many different kinds of fossils do you see in this rock?"

"Bunches, if we include the little ones. But there are, two...no, three big ones. Two invertebrates and a vertebrate. We can make out the tiny ones with my magnifier." She held out the magnifying lens dangling about her neck on a pink shoelace.

"Can you tell me what the bigger ones are?"

"Sure, Grandpa." Jessica pointed to one of many round fossils with a hole in their center. "This one here is a crinoid segment. A crinoid is a sea animal without a backbone. They look kinda like flowers and stay in one place, like flowers do. This rock is very old limestone, so this crinoid died before the dinosaurs were around. You showed me pictures of living ones in your biology books. And do you remember the fossil crinoid at the museum, with all the parts together? Arctic-ulated. Articulated."

Her grandpa couldn't help but smile. "Yes," he said, "I remember it." She knew what she was talking about.

Jessica pointed to another fossil with a determined little index finger. "And these are sponge spicules. Really neat pieces of sponge skeleton. They look kinda like tiny basket weaving. A sponge is an invertebrate."

"That's right." Pointing to another, Jason said, "And what are these?"

"Those are fish scales. A fish is a vertebrate, it has a backbone."
"And how do you know all this, smarty pants?"
"It's all your fault, Grandpa. You made me the fossils set, where I learned about it."
"About what?"
"About paleontology, silly."

The infrared work wound up a dead end, though Daniel's stereo still occasionally turned itself on—even after buying a second, identical receiver. He had just started pursuing a new research angle when, after only three months, his father passed away. With that, Dan just gave up the project altogether. He had failed his father, and there was no way to make up for it.

Chapter 2

Three years later, the tables had turned.

It was winter and cold, but there was no snow on the ground. It was their third night out, and their third cemetery. They were too far out of town to worry about the authorities interfering.

The dark panel-van left the highway and turned onto a county road, following the cemetery sign. Jerry Sterling was driving. Dan was in the passenger seat wearing a heavy jacket and a stocking cap that covered the hair-loss caused by his chemo—he looked about like he felt, pretty awful.

Jerry brought them to a stop just outside the cemetery. He killed the lights and followed the cemetery's gravel drive to the far side of the grounds, where he parked the van with the driver's side facing away from the main road.

Jerry jumped out and headed toward the back of the vehicle. Dan undid his seatbelt and, with some effort, made his way back into the cargo area.

Jerry asked, "What makes you think it'll work tonight?"

"It has to work, Jerry—it just has to! As lousy as I feel, I don't know how much longer I can do this."

Jerry opened the back doors of the van and hauled out a long apparatus that looked rather like a giant, cylindrical bristle brush. He toted the thing to the driver's side of the van, where he fastened it to brackets mounted low, on the rocker panel. When it was secure, Jerry plugged its dangling electrical lead into a nearby receptacle. Finally, he uncovered a neon sign that sprawled across that side of the van.

Jerry returned to the back doors and said, "Okay, it's ready. I still don't get what's so important about using neon."

Dan was sitting at a control console in the van's cargo area. "Actually, it's argon we're using, but generically it's *neon*. There's something weird about neon light at very short wavelengths. We barely see it, but these guys, they're drawn to it like moths to a glaring spotlight." Dan reached for a switch, "Here goes."

Jerry stepped away from the doors and watched as the neon letters flickered to life, in a purple so deep that their glow would have faded to invisibility at any great distance. The sign hummed, as neon always did. Jerry moved further back to take in the full effect. The letters stood out in eerie relief, as if floating in space. They read: "LAST CHANCE FOR THE DEAD TO SPEAK"

The end was near, of that Dan was certain. He just knew that was why Kravitz had called him down to the hospital. And an end had to come. One had to come at last if he were going to pull off that final test, that final experiment, the one he feared most of all. The one that could take place only after his death (not that Daniel had any choice in the matter).

But with the success of last night's test, he couldn't help being excited. All he needed was one more week, *just one*—and then, either the damned thing would work, or it wouldn't.

Using his cane, Dan walked down the cold, bright corridor and entered the hospital's oncology clinic. At the counter, the young nurse looked up at a man of forty-five, who looked much older than his years. A man who likely shouldn't even be walking on his own, who by then should have given up all hope, like all the others who'd gone before him. Instead, he stood before her smiling. She smiled back and said, "Hi, Mr. Dutton, thanks for coming in. Dr. Kravitz is with another patient at the moment, I'll tell him you're here. He'll see you next."

"Thanks, Trudy." Dan turned and looked around the waiting room for a place to sit. He took a seat next to a young boy of ten wearing a stocking cap. The boy was frowning as he pushed frantically at the controls of a game on his phone. "Hi, Willy."

Without looking up, Willy grinned and said, "Hi, Mr. Dutton." The two of them had spent many hours together in that waiting room over the past six months. Willy jabbed a finger at the reset button. "I give up! Have you played *Monster Bash*? It's a lot harder than I thought. The bad monsters keep killing off the good monsters quicker than my mad scientist can bring them back to life."

"Can't say I have, Willy, but I think Jessica has."

Willy handed Dan his phone. "Why don't you try it? You can't lose any worse than I have."

Dan accepted it willingly. Before long, he was totally absorbed in the game, it was a welcome distraction. Several rather strenuous minutes later, Dan gave it up too. "I see what you mean, Willy. But it's fun."

Dr. Kravitz entered the room from the inner office. Willy nodded in the doctor's direction. Dan looked up, grabbed his cane, and got to his feet. Handing the phone back, he said, "Thanks, Willy, I'll see you later. Hope you figure it out."

"Me too. Say hi to Jessica for me."

"I will."

Dan followed the physician into the adjacent hallway. "Hi, Les. Test results, huh?"

Lester Kravitz was making an effort to be upbeat, "Yep. Come on into my office, Dan."

In the doctor's private office, Dan took a seat in a wing-backed chair facing the desk. Kravitz picked up a printout and leaned against his desk. "Sorry you had to come all the way in here to the clinic, Dan. It's been a hectic day. Had to reschedule all the appointments that I couldn't shift down here. We've had three surgeons hard at it all day—a young girl, six years old. Brain tumor. Doesn't look good."

"I'm sorry, Les."

Kravitz paused and, looking at Dan who was smiling, said, "You're making it hard for me to read anything about your condition through that silly grin of yours, Dan. And I'd bet you're not taking your pills."

"I'm not. I can't afford to be a zombie just now."

"So you're writing again?"

Beaming, Dan replied, "No, it's something else." He was almost unable to contain himself. How could he tell an outsider what he knew? "It's another sort of project. Something more important than my writing. I haven't published anything since, well, you know—my dad."

"What're you up to, Dan?"

"You wouldn't understand, Les. It's something my Dad and I had been working on. Maybe later."

Kravitz shrugged. "I miss your father too. Let me know if you change your mind. By the looks of you, I'd say you know something I don't know."

"Sorry, Les. Like I said, *maybe later*—if I'm lucky."

"Hey, Dan, that's okay. But I'm glad you're feeling better than I'd expected. Hell, Sarah's not with you, is she? I'll bet you even drove yourself all the way down here today."

Still smiling, Dan said nothing, just raised his eyebrows.

"You know better than anyone what's going on; you're the one having to ride this out. God knows I wish we'd been able to operate on your tumor." Kravitz held out the printout. "I made you copies of your test results. I'm glad you're finding reason to smile, Dan, but these say it's going to get worse."

Dan's grin evaporated. He took a deep breath and said, "I knew you were going to say that."

"The new treatment didn't help. I'd hoped to arrest or slow it down, but instead the damned thing's growing faster. And we're flat out of alternatives, like your dad's situation. You'd think we'd have more technology going for us after three years. Hasn't happened.

"I wish I knew how you've managed to stay sharp so far into this. Anyone else in your shoes today would have been—as you say, *a zombie*, bed-ridden, and on morphine. Jesus, Dan—you're a walking wonder, with whatever it is you're doing to negate what's going on. But soon the inevitable is going to happen—you won't be able to hold out much longer. Then I won't have to plead with you to take something for the pain. You'll be begging for it!" He was watching Dan's eyes, now that his smile had faded. The eyes always told the story. "It's pretty bad, isn't it?"

Dan nodded and finally let down his guard. "It is. But I'm not ready, Les. Not yet! I'll call you when I can't take it anymore—when I've finally given up."

Dan's hospital bed was in their spare bedroom. Sarah was standing beside him, holding his hand as tears streamed down her cheeks.

Les Kravitz was standing at the far side of the bed, taking Dan's pulse. "Won't you let me give you something for the pain?"

Dan felt awful, but didn't want to be numbed beyond caring. "No, thanks, Les."

Les walked over to the soulful Jerry Sterling, standing at the bedroom door. Under his breath he whispered, "It can't be long now."

Dan looked up into Sarah's tear-filled eyes and managed a faint smile.

She said, "Oh, Dan!"

"I love you, Sarah, and always will." Dan's breath was failing. "It'll be all right… you'll see. Jerry…Jerry and Jessica know what to do." Dan took a long final breath and slowly exhaled. A minute later, his head slumped to the side.

Sarah said, "Oh, no, Dan! Please, don't go! There's so much I need to say!"

When Dan left his body, his view began to include what the disembodied see, but the living miss.

Dan was now standing on the far side of the bed, looking much better. Beside him stood an older woman holding a calico cat. Marla Culpepper. She was disembodied as well.

Dan was surprised at how things had changed. "Marla?"

Marla smiled as she stroked her cat. "Hi, Danny. We've been waiting for you."

It was a drab, rainy day in the cemetery. A tearful Sarah, nine-year-old Jessica, and Jerry Sterling were standing together after the service. Jessica was holding a single long-stemmed red rose. Sarah nodded to Jessica as she dabbed at her tears with a tissue.

Moments later, Jessica was alone at her father's grave. She placed the rose on the casket and smiled a strange, knowing little smile. The casket began its descent.

Chapter 3

Jessica knew she shouldn't talk about it, and she hadn't—well, not really. It was silly to think her friends and classmates would understand. Still, she longed to have someone to share it all with. Anyone.

Everyone thought they knew what death meant. They didn't. But she knew. And that was the problem. What could she say that they'd believe? Like when her classmate Mickey Winchell's dad died in a car accident. That was that. As far as Mickey was concerned, his dad was gone—dead and gone—for good. And maybe he was.

But it wasn't that way with Jessica's dad. Daddy was dead too—as dead as anyone could be, she'd seen that for herself—but he wasn't gone.

The bell rang and Jessica took a deep breath. She poked a finger at the delete button on her tablet's spelling app and her spelling work disappeared from the screen. It didn't matter, she'd been daydreaming all period.

Her fourth-grade teacher, Mrs. Thompson, a woman in her thirties with abiding patience, clapped her hands to summon her pupils' attention. "Now remember, children, with our June break beginning tomorrow, we need to check our desks for anything that might cause problems while we're gone. We don't want any unpleasant surprises again." Everyone knew what she meant. Several of the children giggled.

At the desk next to Jessica's, red-haired, freckle-faced Mickey Winchell, the subject of their laughter, blushed.

In the seat behind Mickey, Billy Armstrong (big for his age and always the first to make mocking remarks) said, "Yeah, Mickey. If it weren't for you, the world would never know ants will do anything for a cookie" He laughed and poked a finger in Mickey's ribs.

Jessica said, "Keep it to yourself, Billy! If you're so perfect, why do you feel you have to pick on people? You're just being a jerk!"

The grin vanished from Billy's face and he got up to leave.

Jessica told Mickey, "Don't pay any attention to Billy. He just doesn't know any better. Besides, I think it was cool the way those hundreds of little ants came all the way in here to carry off your cookie, one tiny little bite at a time."

"Thanks, Jessica," said Mickey. "I think it was cool too."

Jessica made her way into the coat room to get her lunch box. There she bumped into Sissy Stormer, bright-eyed and excited, who exclaimed,"I just had a brilliant idea, Jessica. Why don't you ride up to camp with Charlotte and me? I know my mom'll have plenty of room for you and your stuff in our van. And it'll save your mom the trip. Besides, we rode with you last year—now it's your turn to ride with us."

Jessica liked Sissy; she was always so bubbly and happy. "Sure, Sissy. I'd like to. Let me ask my mom first, but I think it'll be okay." On their way out of the classroom, Mrs. Thompson caught Jessica's eye and waved her over. Jessica turned to Sissy and said, "I'll call you tonight."

"Okay. Bye." Sissy turned and ran to catch up with Charlotte.

Jessica made her way past the other kids to her teacher. Mrs. Thompson said, "Jessica, Mrs. Flood requested that I have you come and see her after school. She's waiting for you."

Jessica looked stricken. She swallowed hard and asked, "Mrs. Flood wants to see me? Now?" She fiddled with her lunch box and a paper sack full of things she was taking home over the break. "But I'll miss my bus, Mrs. Thompson. I can't miss my bus! I've got to get home to get ready for camp tomorrow."

"That won't be a problem, honey. Mrs. Flood said she'd see that you got a ride. You'll probably arrive home before your bus."

Reluctantly, Jessica gave in and said, "Okay, thank you." She'd been afraid it might come to this. Maybe she should call home and ask her mother what to do—then she remembered—no, she couldn't. Besides, if Mrs. Flood was waiting for her, she couldn't afford to make things worse by being late.

Mrs. Thompson was concerned at Jessica's perceived plight. "There's nothing wrong, Jessica. You haven't a thing to worry about. Mrs. Flood is as concerned about you as I am."

Maybe Mrs. Thompson was someone Jessica could confide in, she liked her a lot. But she would never understand. No one would.

"Would you like me to go with you to Mrs. Flood's office? I'd be glad to."

"No. It's okay, but thank you for offering."

"All right, honey, if you're certain. But I'll be here for a while still, if you change your mind. And if I don't see you again today, you have a nice time at camp."

Jessica started backing down the hall toward the principal's office and said, "Thanks, I hope you have a nice break too, Mrs. Thompson."

"Good-bye, Jessica." Mrs. Thompson watched as forlorn Jessica Dutton made her way down the hall and around the corner. She felt guilty for having ruined Jessica's day, as if the child didn't have enough to deal with already—Jessica had been happy. What business did she have interfering in someone else's grief, when she couldn't cope with her own? And now she'd complicated Jessica's life by talking to Mrs. Flood about her. She wanted to call Jessica back. But it was too late.

Mrs. Flood was waiting for Jessica, but she wasn't cross like Jessica had feared. Maybe it was because she had company in her office—a pretty lady with long blonde hair, wearing a flowered dress. The lady got to her feet as Jessica entered the office.

Mrs. Flood introduced her by saying, "Jessica, this is Mrs. Raymond. She works with the school district. Mrs. Raymond was hoping she could have a short visit with you."

"Hello," said Jessica, tentatively.

Mrs. Raymond smiled warmly and said, "Hello, Jessica." She asked Mrs. Flood, "Can we get Jessica a chair?"

"Certainly," said Mrs. Flood, as she left the room in search of a chair.

Mrs. Raymond tried to reassure Jessica, "There's no reason for you to be worried, honey. I'd just like to speak with you for a few minutes, if that's okay with you?"

Jessica nodded. "I...I guess so." Mrs. Flood returned with a chair and placed it near her guest. Jessica seated herself.

They sat silent for a moment. Finally, Mrs. Raymond leaned toward Jessica and in a hushed voice said, "We're concerned, Jessica, about how you've been doing. Your teacher and Mrs. Flood have been worried about you. They haven't been able to reach your mother and don't have a work number for her. Is everything okay at home?"

Jessica didn't know what to say and didn't want to say the wrong thing. Mrs. Raymond seemed nice and genuinely concerned, but what could she say? "Well, I... everything is fine."

"Are you sure?"

Jessica hesitated, then said, "Yes," more sure of herself this time.

"Does your mother work, Jessica? Is there any way we can reach her this afternoon?"

"She works—she runs my father's business."

Mrs. Raymond raised her eyebrows. "Wasn't your father a writer?"

"Yes, he was a writer, but royalties are still coming in, and he has...uh, he left several manuscripts to be published. So my mother works in my father's office. He called it his office. It's really his den."

"Could we reach her there now?"

"No!" Jessica blurted out. "My father hardly ever answered the phone during the day. He said he 'couldn't write and run telephone central at the same time.' So my mother doesn't answer it either. She checks for messages in the evening. If I have an emergency, I can call our neighbor, Mrs. Milovski—'Mrs. M.,' we call her. She walks over and tells my mother. Mrs. M. doesn't mind. Her father was a writer too, so she understands. Mrs. M. is out of town this week; her brother is having gallbladder surgery." Jessica was proud of herself—it was all true.

"Jessica, do you think your mother would mind if I came home with you after school to talk?"

Jessica was stunned. She hadn't imagined any such possibility. And for the same reasons she'd given Mrs. Raymond, she had no way of giving her mother any warning.

"Do you think it'd be all right, Jessica?" Jessica didn't answer. She must have looked as numb as she felt. Mrs. Raymond reached over and placed her hand on Jessica's. "Jessica, do you think your mother would mind?"

"Huh? Oh, I don't know, Mrs. Raymond. I...I don't know." But she knew.

"Why don't we just try, honey? I don't think your mother will really mind. Is that okay with you?"

From way off somewhere, Jessica heard herself say, "I guess so."

Mrs. Raymond was nice and somehow Jessica knew that this lady was doing what she felt was right and correct—if she'd only known.

Jessica didn't say a thing all the way home, except to give directions. She was certain that anything else she'd say would just make things worse, so the safest thing to do was to say nothing.

As they approached her home, Jessica pointed and said, "This is it." Mrs. Raymond turned and parked in the Duttons' driveway.

At the front door Jessica rang the doorbell. A few moments later, her mother opened the door. "Oh my gosh, Jessica, it's you! What have you...?"

"Mom," said Jessica, "This is Mrs. Raymond."

The women shook hands.

"Please call me Judy. I'm sorry, Mrs. Dutton, this is all my doing. I'm a social worker with the Albuquerque School District. I hope this isn't a problem."

"Uh, no," said Sarah. "It's no problem at all. I thought. I thought Jessica had missed her bus. She never rings the doorbell. Come on in, Judy." Sarah gestured for Judy to enter.

As they entered, the Dutton's collie, Terra, added her greeting, "Woof!"

Jessica stroked Terra's head. "Mom, can I go over to Charlotte's and help her get ready for camp?"

"Sure. If you're not gone too long."

"Thanks, Mom. Charlotte can help me with my stuff when we're done."

"Well, I don't know if that's necessary."

Jessica reached for the door latch, then hesitated. "I almost forgot. Sissy asked if I could ride to camp with her and Charlotte tomorrow." She waved to Judy Raymond and said, "It was nice meeting you." Then she and the collie zoomed out the door and were gone. The screen door slammed shut behind them.

Judy chuckled and said, "She's a lovely child."

Sarah led Judy toward the back of the house. On the way, they passed dozens of postal trays filled with mail. Sarah led her through the French doors and out to their garden.

They stopped near the zinnias, not far from a gurgling waterfall. "What is it that I can do for you, Judy?"

"It's Jessica. They—well, her teacher, and now the school principal, are concerned about how she's doing. How she's doing since her father's death."

"Why didn't her teacher call me?"

"I wondered about that too, until I learned that her teacher, Mrs. Thompson, had just recently lost her own father."

"Oh, I see."

"The school principal called me in. She feels Jessica's having trouble adjusting to her father's death."

"Really?"

"It has been four months," said Judy. "It might have amounted to nothing otherwise, but she speaks of her father like, well—like he's still alive. It's been unsettling to the other children. Parents have called."

"I see what you mean."

Embarrassed in needing to mention it, Judy said, "The district could recommend a counselor—if you felt that was appropriate."

Sarah sighed and looked away, gathering her thoughts. After a long pause, she finally, though still reluctantly, said, "We knew it would come to this, Judy. You're the first." Sarah motioned toward a nearby garden bench. "This might be easier sitting down." They made their way to the bench. "I honestly don't know where to begin, but here goes—Jessica is correct in speaking of her father in the present tense."

Judy's eyes widened. "What are you saying?"

"He's still with us."

Judy nodded uneasily, and asked, "You mean that figuratively, of course?"

"No," said Sarah. "Quite literally." Sarah paused, waiting for some sign that Judy understood. Judy was staring into space. Sarah continued anyway. "Dan was trying to enable a person to communicate with the living after his own death."

Judy still didn't respond.

"It was a project he and his father, Dr. Jason Dutton, had worked on together."

That brought Judy around. "Jason Dutton was your father-in-law? Oh, my gosh! I don't know why I didn't make the connection. His book was amazing! I've read all of your husband's books too. I'm so sorry!"

"Thank you, Judy. As you might have noticed inside, we've gotten thousands of letters of condolence."

Judy continued, "I especially loved your husband's last book, *Electric Seance*. It was—oh, my gosh—it was about the same subject. You're really serious!" Judy grabbed her purse, leapt to her feet, and fainted. Sarah jumped up, caught Judy in mid-fall, and set her down gently on the garden walk.

A few moments later, Judy was coming around. When she opened her eyes, Sarah said, "You fainted."

"I did? I...I haven't fainted since—since we lost Penny."

"I'm sorry, Judy."

"It's okay. It's just, it's just that sometimes—when I think about Penny, or my mom —I feel strange, like what just happened."

"Let's get you somewhere where it's more comfortable." Sarah helped Judy to her feet and over to a chaise lounge on the patio. "Can I get you something to drink, maybe some fruit juice?"

"That would be great. I didn't eat lunch today."

"No wonder! I'll fix you a sandwich too."

Twenty minutes later, Judy was herself again. "I don't know what it means, but your husband's last book meant so much to me. So much! Because Penny, our two-year-old, came back after we lost her, to say goodbye. I've never told anyone the rest —not even my husband, Gil. When I told him Penny had come back, he mocked me. He laughed at me. Our relationship hasn't been the same since. It was humiliating. I didn't dare share the rest—that Penny had held my hand, my fingers, with her little hands like she always did and said, 'I love you, Mommy.' It was so sweet. So real. So wonderful!

"I'd read *Electric Seance* the year before. I knew your husband's story was supposed to be fiction, but then with his Author's Note—it made my experience seem so utterly real. Have you ever read a book that put you in an altered state?"

"I have," said Sarah. "I know exactly what you mean."

"Well, your husband's book did that for me. It prepared me for what was to come. I'm so thankful for his work—and his father's book, years before, while I was still in college. Between the two of them, they've made such a huge difference in my life. Penny wasn't the first. My mother had come to me the night of her plane crash, before I even knew she was dead."

Sarah told her about the incident with the stereo—how it had led Dan to eventually develop something like the technology in his novel.

"You know, Judy, you could actually speak with Dan, if you wanted. His best friend, Jerry, is the only other person who knows about what Dan has accomplished. Jerry helped with the project along the way. I know Dan would love adding you to our tiny circle of friends in the know—because this is real to you!"

"Honestly?" asked Judy. "Oh, that would be so wonderful!" Judy was ecstatic. "Maybe I could—this is unreal. Maybe I could, could talk with him about his books. And his father. I never knew my father—he died before I was born. And like I said, I lost my mom when I was away at college—just after I'd read Jason Dutton's wonderful book, exactly when I needed it. After the book, and losing my mom, I sort of saw him as a father figure—a very wise, knowing father who understood the really important things. I've read *DEAD, BUT NOT GONE* at least a dozen times.

"And you know—oh my gosh!" added Judy. "Things happen for a reason. I think—I really do—I think I've been on a journey preparing me *for this!* Here! Today! My job —my experiences—all have been important steps in leading me right here!"

"I know Dan would love visiting with you; he's so like his father. They were very close."

"I would absolutely love speaking with him, visiting with him. But could we do it another day? I'm so all-in emotionally just now. I really have to get home, I... Gil will be waiting for me. I don't want... Could we do it one evening next week? Maybe Wednesday, at seven o'clock?"

"That would be perfect. Wednesday at seven it is. I know Dan will look forward to it."

Sarah enjoyed visiting with Judy—such a sweet open young woman. It *had* been an emotional day for her. Sarah walked Judy to her car. "Are you absolutely certain you feel well enough to drive? I'd be glad to give you a ride home."

Judy climbed into her car, and started the engine. "I'm fine now—really! Thank you so much, Sarah. I'm looking forward to next Wednesday. We all need someone to share the important things with, someone with whom it's okay to be yourself." Judy waved and said, "Good-bye," as she pulled away.

Sarah headed back to the house. She entered from the foyer, reclined on the living room sofa, and covered her eyes with her hands. "If I'd only returned the school's calls, she'd never have just shown up like this."

A male voice came from a small loudspeaker sitting on the coffee table, "You were perfect, honey. But Judy's husband sure is a major disappointment." Invisible to Sarah, a disembodied Daniel Dutton was sitting in the adjacent armchair.

"*Disappointment* is being way too kind, Dan. But I didn't have to just drop all this on her like I did."

"Maybe," said Dan, again through the speaker. "But this was going to happen sooner or later. At least it was with someone receptive, a sweet, young woman who actually needs us. Could've been much worse. And you were right, we should add to our 'tiny circle of friends in the know.' It's time."

Sarah sat up. "Do you think she'll do something? Maybe say something to some jerk like her husband?"

Daniel smiled, Sarah had a way with words. "I don't know. I guess we'll see."

"I know what to do," said Sarah, "I'll talk with Jerry in the morning. When he's back from Phoenix."

While Sarah and Judy were talking, a small dark form had been skittering about the garden, back and forth, out of sight. It darted behind huge flower pots, up and down trees, under bushes, among the various flower beds, and around the vegetable garden. Several times the high-pitched hum of an approaching mosquito had been cut short as it was perforated in midair by a needle-thin laser beam.

Sarah and Judy's benefactor, Ned, was good at what he did. Daniel Dutton liked to say he had *just tinkered Ned together*, a phrase he'd borrowed from one of his favorite classic sci-fi films.

The nimble little pest and weed-controlling automaton looked rather like a squirrel, albeit a pop-eyed, metallic squirrel with laser weapons and a focused water cannon strapped to its back.

It had long been known that insects dowsed with soapy water died of asphyxiation in seconds—a fact the agri-chemical manufacturers ignored when advertising their hazardous alternatives. Ned's innovation was that such a stream of water, when aimed very precisely, did the trick with little expense, no collateral damage to beneficial species, and no harm to the environment. His lasers were never aimed at anything other than cold-blooded creatures.

Weeds were plucked from the ground as seedlings—the few that got as far as actual germination. Generally, Ned collected the unwanted seeds he found, ground them to a pulp in his gullet, after which they continued on to his false stomach— where their heat of decomposition assisted in recharging his batteries. The odd individual weed that reached any size, was neatly cut short with Ned's little rotary saw and dragged to the compost pile.

Dan had long since sold all manufacturing license to his creation (though he still owned the basic patents), saying he'd 'Rather write and take a percentage than sweat the small stuff, as long as the technology wasn't about to go off the rails.'

It hadn't taken long for Ned's siblings to become commonplace inhabitants of urban gardens and such, ultimately becoming almost as numerous as squirrels in affluent neighborhoods; a single unit had proven more than adequate for the average yard. Dan had dubbed them *Garden Guardians*. It had taken only a few years for the economies of scale in manufacturing to make the little automatons cheaper to employ than applying their environmentally-undesirable chemical alternatives.

On the day of Judy's visit, Dan's original prototype of the device had truncated the life cycles of a great many invertebrate undesirables. Among his targets had been squash bugs and cucumber beetles dining in the vegetable garden, crickets and grasshoppers, and scores of tiny black ants attempting an incursion into the Dutton kitchen.

The creatures Ned was programmed to ignore or protect—bees, wasps, butterflies, moths, flower flies, mantises, lady bugs, non-venomous spiders, and particular larval forms, all of them invertebrate allies of man—had pretty much free rein of the premises. Ned kept a running inventory of the creatures. His domain included their gardens, trees and shrubs—and he took whatever action might be necessary to further his mission.

Ned's somewhat tortoise-shaped relative, Gus, saw to it that the front lawn was maintained at its proper length—while weeds, ticks, fleas, and the like were kept under strict control.

In the seven intervening years, Ned and his kind had essentially eliminated the need for insecticides and weed control in urban applications, and they were making significant inroads into commercial agriculture. It seemed likely that the use of chemical pesticides and herbicides might cease altogether within the next few years, given that the largest of the agricultural chemical companies had hedged their bets and invested heavily in the technology.

Chapter 4

A BMW pulled into the parking lot next to Jerry Sterling's office building. Jerry exited the car and started walking toward his office.

Sarah hopped out of her car, parked at the nearby curb, and yelled, "Jerry!"

Jerry turned. "Sarah? What are you doing here?"

She ran up to him. "Can we talk? Can we go somewhere and talk? I think we're in trouble!"

"What's going on?"

"It's happened, Jerry. It's finally happened. They know about Dan!"

"Christ! How'd that happen?" Jerry looked around for a place to talk. "Let's get a cup of coffee." He grabbed Sarah's arm and guided her through the morning traffic toward the diner across the street.

They entered the diner, Jerry held up two fingers for the waitress behind the counter, and then steered Sarah to a booth. The waitress almost beat them there with their cups of coffee. Jerry winked and said, "Thanks, Betty."

Sarah began her explanation, "A doctor from the psych center called and wants to talk with me."

"What? What's the deal?"

"Well, Jessica brought home a social worker from the school district. One thing led to another—and now they know."

Loud enough for the entire diner to hear him, Jerry said, "What's a shrink got to do with it?"

Sarah leaned closer and whispered, "Geez, Jerry!" She put a finger to her lips to quiet him down. "I was telling Judy, the girl from the school district, about Dan and…"

"You, what? Christ, Sarah. You just told her point blank?"

"What else could I do?" She looked around to see if others were still listening. "Now her doctor, Dr. Smithson, says Judy suffered an emotional collapse. She was fine when she left our place. I feel so bad; she's such a sweet girl."

"Wow, Sarah! When you do something, you sure do it up right."

"Thanks, Jer. Anyway—Dan would like you to be there when the doctor shows up tonight."

Dr. Joseph Smithson, a man in his sixties, was finishing off a French pastry as he pulled into the Dutton's driveway.

Moments later, the doorbell rang. Sarah rushed to answer it.

"Mrs. Dutton? I'm Joseph Smithson. Thank you for agreeing to see me."

"Hello, Doctor. Please come in." Sarah led Smithson into their living room, where Jerry was waiting. Dan was standing in the kitchen doorway.

"Dr. Smithson, this is our attorney, Jerry Sterling."

Jerry offered his hand. "My pleasure, Doctor."

"The pleasure is mine, Mr. Sterling."

Sarah said, "Why don't we have a seat?"

Jerry pulled out a pocket recorder and said, "I hope you don't mind my recording our conversation, Doctor."

"Certainly not, Mr. Sterling. If I may retain freedom to share anecdotal information with my professional colleagues."

Jerry replied, "That will be possible, but only if we are assured of the utmost discretion from you and your colleagues."

"Absolutely. You have my word."

"I hope you're up to this, Doctor!"

"So do I, Mr. Sterling."

Sarah just decided to jump in. "What do you need to know, Doctor?"

"I'd like to know what occurred yesterday—regarding your meeting with Judy Raymond."

"Well, she had come to discuss my daughter's behavior at school. I thought Judy was doing pretty well when she left here. She was enthusiastic about our visiting again."

"Really? Then perhaps something happened afterward. I didn't see her at the hospital until 8:00 P.M., when her husband brought her in."

"Her husband brought her in?"

"He did."

"How strange. Judy fainted during our discussion in the garden. But she came around soon enough."

"Fainted?"

"Yes, Doctor. We talked at length afterward. By the time she left, she seemed fine. Oh, there's something else. She's afraid of her husband."

"Afraid? Is that what she said?"

"Not exactly, but he had mocked her when she was very vulnerable. After their child's death. She had had an experience the previous night, a very real and meaningful experience for Judy, but she made the mistake of sharing some of it with her husband. And I don't know how else to describe it, Doctor—but he laughed at her, he humiliated her so completely, that she held back the remainder of her experience.

"She was happy when she left here yesterday afternoon, happy that at last she had someone to share her stories with. Someone who understood. I don't know, but perhaps she had another such upset with her husband after leaving here."

Dr. Smithson sat silently, taking it all in.

"Maybe she tried to share our talk with her husband. Maybe he beat her down again, emotionally. You said her husband brought her to the hospital. That could mean something. Like I said, she's afraid of him. Don't they question people when they come to the E.R., about whether or not they feel safe at home?"

"You're right, they do look for abuse. But Judy was pretty much incoherent last night. He did most of the talking. I'd seen her about a year ago, just after the death of their daughter. Judy was relatively together back then, but needed some help dealing with the loss. I don't recall any indications she was being abused, though that doesn't mean she wasn't. Last night, like I said, he did most of the talking; he wanted to have her committed."

"Committed? You're kidding me."

"I agreed to admit her to the hospital as a psychiatric patient, so she could rest, and ultimately be evaluated. I made it clear to him that she couldn't be committed on his say-so."

"That sweet girl is as sane as you or me, Doctor. If you ask me, it's her husband who should be evaluated. Judy doesn't dare be herself with him. She was afraid of getting home late, like he had her on a very short leash."

"Perhaps you have something there, Sarah. When I told him that a judge would have to sign any commitment papers, he was very put off."

"I don't want her brutalized further by her husband," said Sarah. "She's a very sweet and caring young woman, very much in need of someone with whom she can be herself. Her husband is not that person. He's more like her master, her tormentor. You should have seen how she lit up when I shared what's been going on in our lives."

"And that," said Smithson, "brings us back to my reason for speaking with you this evening. I want to do what's best for Judy, but I need to understand. You said that she fainted, while you were discussing your daughter's school behavior. What were you saying when that occurred?"

"Well," said Sarah. "She was asking about Jessica's remarks to her classmates."

"What remarks?'

"I don't know specifically what Jessica has said—but she apparently gave her classmates the impression that her father was still a part of her life."

"But your husband is deceased."

"Yes, Doctor. Dan passed away four months ago."

"I'm so sorry for your loss, Sarah. He'll be sorely missed by his many fans, myself among them. And I knew his father, Jason."

"His father was a wonderful man."

"Yes, one of a kind," said Smithson. I'm sorry, I'm rather taking us off the subject."

"Yes, Doctor, but it's all good." said Sarah, not particularly anxious to be getting to the subject of his visit.

"And so—Judy asked you about your daughter's remarks at school, remarks sounding rather like her deceased father was still a part of her life. Is that true?"

Sarah pulled herself together, sat up, and declared, "It is."

"And what did you say that upset Judy so?"

"Well, I was trying to tell her about Dan's interface."

"Interface?"

"The device he created. It's how we still talk with him."

"You talk with him? Really? Certainly it's common knowledge that he was a successful engineer and a renowned inventor, in addition to his writing career. But what you're claiming is…"

"Fantastic!"

"Yes. 'Fantastic!'" said Smithson. "And much more, to put it mildly."

"None the less, Doctor—it's true."

Smithson thought a long moment, looking absently out a nearby window, then turned back to Sarah and said, "And when you shared this with Judy Raymond, that's when she fainted?"

"Yes, Doctor."

"All right. For the sake of argument, I'll attempt to just suspend my disbelief of your assertion and ask you how often this communication occurs? Are there any particular circumstances or phenomena when it happens?"

"Phenomena? Circumstances? It occurs constantly, Doctor."

"And has it happened today?"

"Of course! All day—every day."

Smithson shivered when he asked, "And is your husband in this room with us now?"

After a long pause, a voice from the loudspeaker on the coffee table said, "I am." Dan was now in his favorite chair near the sofa and coffee table.

Smithson jumped and pointed when he said, "Did...did that come from this speaker?"

Sarah just grinned.

Not buying it, Smithson said, "Is this disembodied voice that of a ghost, or are you pulling my leg?"

The voice from the speaker said, "Do you see the smartphone on the coffee table next to this speaker?"

"I do!"

"Well," said Dan, "let's just say—I'm a dead guy with an edge."

"I'm not certain I understand. Is this Daniel Dutton I'm speaking with?"

"The one and only!"

Smithson looked around the room. He got to his feet and, rather cautiously, checked out the kitchen, and then the hallway at the opposite end of the living room. "How do I know I'm not speaking with someone talking into a microphone from another room?"

"Good question," said Dan. "I guess you'll have to figure that one out for yourself, Doctor."

"Hmmm," said Smithson, still looking around the front of the house and behind the living room furniture for some clue as to what was going on. "An interesting problem." Having exhausted his search of the immediate area, Smithson said, "All right..." He looked out the front window, toward the driveway and his car. "If you're a disembodied spirit, then you should be able to tell me what I have sitting on the back seat of my car." Smithson, still standing, kept an eye on his car. It was approaching twilight, but it was obvious, at least as seen from his current vantage point, that there was no one anywhere near the vehicle.

Dan said, "Well, let's see." Dan's ghostly image, unseen by the trio, walked toward the closed front door and passed right through it.

A few moments later, Dan reappeared precisely where he had been seated earlier. "I'm back."

Smithson flinched.

"You have a book on the back seat—*WINNIE THE POOH*. There's also a stuffed animal—an elephant. As far as the rest of the car goes, you have several French pastries in a sack on the front passenger seat. In the trunk, there are three files in your briefcase for the same patient. The name is Vernon Reynolds. He has a history of insomnia, but when he does sleep, he has recurring nightmares about his father's fatal hunting accident."

Smithson finally took his seat on the sofa. "Unbelievable!"

Dan continued, "The elephant and book, each nicely wrapped, are for your granddaughter, Becky. Her birthday is tomorrow."

"I don't know that any of this proves that you're dead," said Smithson, "but it's absolutely remarkable! It's amazing, especially about the patient files—and the wrapped gifts."

"Regarding the gifts' purpose," said Dan, "I'm just reading your thoughts, Doctor. For some reason I can often, though not always, pick up the thoughts, the mental images, of those in my vicinity."

"Unbelievable!" remarked Smithson.

Sarah chimed in, "Our daughter, Jessica, hears Dan without the interface—and sees him."

Smithson didn't know what to think. He shook his head and said, "I don't know. If what you're saying is true, it changes everything. What exactly is this interface you mentioned?"

Dan said, "The device connected to the bottom of this phone, the dongle, it's the interface. The software running it is an app installed on the phone."

Smithson leaned forward and reached for the phone. "May I?"

"Certainly, Doctor."

Smithson picked up the phone and touched the dongle that hung from its base. It looked much like a flexible bottlebrush and was about three inches long. "Fascinating. Is there any reason why others in your condition couldn't use this device?"

"None. It's very straight-forward. It functions rather intuitively in place of the neural interface between the human brain and the body's vocal mechanism. It's easier to adapt to than one might think—just a few minutes to settle into its eccentricities. It feels very much like the circuitry in a living body. I just grab it, spiritually, and it works."

Sarah added, "Jessica decided it looks like a foxtail, so that's what we've started calling it."

Smithson asked, "Are you planning to release this technology to the public?"

"Eventually, I suppose. If nothing unpleasant occurs after tonight."

Jerry jumped in, "But let us warn you, Doctor. The device self-destructs if tampered with. It would avail one nothing to obtain it by force or theft."

"I understand, Mr. Sterling. And I see the necessity for caution. Why, in the wrong hands…"

"Yes," said Dan. "*In the wrong hands*, it could be used to enslave. Believe me, with its potential for ill, it is my responsibility to see that it is used solely for good. Or I will have to destroy it—utterly and for all time!"

Dan's biggest disappointment, after his own demise, was that his father was nowhere to be found—not among the dead, at least. He felt certain his dad would have waited for him, if he could, and perhaps just hung around for a time following the lives of those who survived him. Of course, there'd been three years in-between—years during which his father must have moved on.

Dan's world, the world of the dead, wasn't anything like one would have expected from literature, or film. *Bizarre* would have been too sedate an adjective. Certainly, he was aware of other disembodied spirits like himself—some few were, for lack of a better term, stuck in the events or places of their demise, as ghosts.

The majority of the others of his kind, very soon after death, just left for parts unknown—only to return later in a singleminded panic to just jump back onto the carousel of life. Dan vowed that one day, he'd follow one of them to discover the how, what, and where of the goings-on in-between.

There were still a significant number of the newly-dead who just hung around, as he did, trying to make sense of it all—if there were any real sense to be made. And there were a few who just would not take no for an answer. They more than anything wanted to go back, back with the living, and they did.

The world around Daniel, the universe itself, was literally crawling with spirits. The old adage, *walls have ears*, was no exaggeration. Not just *ears*, but eyes as well, and feelings, even opinions.

Everything, everywhere, was suffused in no small part with spirits, or remnants of their passing—much like fossils were remnants of past life in the corporeal world.

Chapter 5

"What idiot put Smithson on this case?" shrieked Dr. Ernest Feemish. To the staff of the university hospital and its psychiatric center, he was "Dr. Not-so-Earnest Feemish." Certainly, he was the director of the Psychiatric Department, and it was common opinion that he might more appropriately be dubbed "the establishment's number one patient."

Feemish continued his rant, "First thing this morning, I learned that Smithson had an interview with a dead man. Why on earth would anyone write a serious report on such a thing? This is so like Smithson. Fortunately, I acquired a copy before the entire world had seen it. Unfortunately, so did Malcolm Claridge. What the hell is this place coming to?"

The unfortunate individual on the receiving end of Feemish's tirade was clinical psychologist Julian Frost. Up until then, Frost had held up pretty well under Feemish's assaults, but his skin was wearing thin. If he were lucky, Feemish would soon blow a gasket and give them all some much deserved relief. Reluctantly, Frost lowered his shield and left himself open for another barrage. "Smithson is highly thought of, sir. I'm told that it's his name alone on our federal grant requests that has kept us head and shoulders above the other teaching hospitals in the region."

"You think so? Well I'll be the judge of that! Now listen to me, Julian. I have a meeting with Malcolm Claridge at three this afternoon. I need Smithson there with me—Claridge wants a first-hand report. I'll be damned if I can say why he would have any interest in such nonsense."

"I'll do what I can, sir. But I understand that Smithson is scheduled to be at his practice all day today."

"You arrange it, Julian, whatever it takes. If there's one thing I've learned at this university, it's that you don't cross Malcolm Claridge. Why without the Claridge

Foundation, this school's claim to fame would likely be something like dairy science—certainly not medicine. You may not be aware of the fact, having been on campus only a few months now, but those who have crossed Claridge no longer work in their chosen fields. He's not a man to be taken lightly. Get the picture?"

"Yes, sir. I'll see that Smithson is at Claridge's office at three sharp, if I have to carry him there myself."

The Claridge Foundation was an imposing, classically-styled twenty-story building in downtown Albuquerque.

Joseph Smithson stepped off the elevator and entered the anteroom of Claridge's office.

Feemish was there waiting for him. The man bolted out of his chair. "Oh my Lord, Smithson! I thought you'd let me down. I was already trying to decide what to do after I cleaned out my desk. I've never been so glad to see anyone in my life!"

"I'm sorry I gave you a turn, Ernest. All's well—I'm here."

Claridge's assistant stepped up and said, "Mr. Claridge will see you now, Dr. Smithson." To Feemish she said, "Thank you, Dr. Feemish. Perhaps we'll see you another time."

"He doesn't want to see me? Oh, my gosh! Thank you. Thank you so very much!" He shook Smithson's hand and said, "Bless you, Joseph!" And was gone.

The assistant guided Smithson toward a door just beyond, led him through a spacious library, and finally past a heavy oak door that she closed behind him.

The room was dimly-lit and smelled of wintergreen and cigar smoke. The contrast in light levels, between the bright library and this adjoining room, left Smithson unable to make out his new surroundings. As his eyes finally adjusted, he could identify the presence before him. He knew the man, but one couldn't call them friends. Claridge, a corpulent man in his late sixties, was seated behind a huge desk. He waved Smithson over to a nearby chair.

"Joseph," Claridge offered his hand. "I read the report you submitted on the Dutton interview—an excellent report." Joseph shook the man's hand and sat down. "If you've interpreted this correctly," Claridge hefted a printout of Smithson's account, "this is a most amazing discovery."

"I'm glad you agree," said Smithson, who was visibly disappointed that Claridge had a copy of his account, for the man was not an intended recipient. Smithson made a mental note to query the few professional contacts with whom he'd shared his rendition of the Dutton interview.

Claridge puffed at his cigar. "You'd find out soon enough, Joseph, so I'll admit that I've intercepted your report."

Smithson jumped to his feet. "You what?"

"I have one of only two copies."

"Why, and more importantly, how? How have you intercepted my correspondence?"

Ignoring Smithson's indignation, Claridge continued, "This material is too sensitive to be released at this time."

"Sensitivity be damned, Malcolm. You have no business interfering in my professional affairs. If you think your position as one of the medical school's benefactors gives you a right to suppress legitimate communication between staff physicians. Why this innovation's importance is exactly why I must share it with my professional peers."

Still unruffled, Claridge went on. "You'll see the sense of this soon enough, Joseph."

"Don't *Joseph* me, Malcolm. This sort of interference will not stand."

Claridge kept at it. "What's the situation with this..." he picked up the report and read the girl's name, "Judy Raymond?"

Incensed, a pacing Smithson spat out his response to Claridge. "She's coming off sedation."

"How unfortunate. How many others know about this?" He jabbed a finger at the printout on his desk.

Smithson gave a look that said he knew what Claridge was up to. "With your interception of my report, there are only the Duttons, their attorney, Judy Raymond, and myself."

"Good. And then, of course, there's Feemish. Ah, well, no worries." Claridge picked up the ornate humidor on his desk, raised its lid, and held it out to Smithson. "Try one, Joseph."

Still livid, Smithson refused the offer, "No, thank you."

Claridge lit a cigar and puffed its tip to a healthy glow. "It's your loss, Joseph. These are lovely Havanas."

Joseph turned to leave.

"Oh," said Claridge, "One more thing..."

Getting Claridge's drift, Joseph spun around and said, "Forget it, Malcolm. Stealing the device would be futile. It self-destructs if tampered with."

"I see." Claridge set down his cigar. "Now listen here, Joseph. I'd like you to agree to keep this information to yourself, for the time being at least. And I feel, that at least for now, further contact with the Duttons is unwise."

Again, Smithson turned to leave. He grabbed the door knob, stared Claridge in the eye, and said, "I'll make you no such guarantees," then stormed out of the room, slamming the door.

Later that night, in the psychiatric ward of the university medical center, Russ Carver approached Judy Raymond's hospital room. In his late thirties, Carver was tall and fit, with a short ragged beard and slicked-back hair. He wore a doctor's lab coat, though he wasn't a doctor, and had a stethoscope dangling about his neck. Unnoticed, Carver entered Judy Raymond's darkened room and closed the door.

Judy was asleep, dreaming.

In her dream, Judy was in her negligee and barefoot, walking happily, as delicate ferns tugged at her ankles and calves. Overhead, the towering ponderosa and sugar pines dwarfed her, blocking all but the occasional bright ray of sunlight. She picked a pine sprig, held it close, and inhaled its fragrance deeply. Judy looked up and the forest began spinning slowly about her, then faster, until finally she fell ever-so-slowly to the soft forest floor.

Back in her hospital room, Judy awoke. Carver was above her, forcing something over her mouth and nose. Judy screamed, but her cries, muffled by the ether-soaked cloth, went unheard. She tried to fight him off, but his upper-body weight was heavy upon her, as one strong hand held both her wrists.

Down the corridor, at the nurse's station, the young nurse behind the counter addressed her older co-worker, who was just returning from the break room, "Did you hear something, Agatha? I thought I heard a voice down that way." She pointed toward Judy's room.

"Nope," said Agatha, "and I won't. Everyone down there is sedated, except 314. And that sweet child is finally off her meds and sleeping like a baby."

In 314 Judy was still resisting, then abruptly went limp. Carver pulled a hypodermic needle from his lab coat pocket, uncovered it, and injected a substance into her neck.

It was Saturday. Sarah was in the kitchen cleaning up after her little breakfast. Jessica was at camp, having departed Thursday morning with her friends. Dan was away for the moment.

Sarah turned from the sink and grabbed her phone from the counter behind her. The device came to life with her touch. Sarah frowned, something was different.

The phone's wallpaper image, the photo of Jessica hugging her collie, was gone. Another picture had taken its place. A flower. A simple, artful drawing of a daisy. Just as if someone had finger-painted the image onto her phone while her back was turned. So odd. So beautifully simple.

But what did it mean?

Later that morning, Joseph Smithson was seated in his car in the hospital parking lot. He was on his cell phone. "Sarah, hi. This is Joseph Smithson. Is there any way I might speak with Daniel?"

"Certainly, Doctor. Just a moment."

Seconds later, Daniel was on the line. "Hello, Joseph."

"Hello, Daniel. There's something I need to tell you—Judy Raymond passed away last night."

"I know," said Daniel.

"You know? How could you?"

"She's here, Doctor. She showed up."

In the background, Sarah added, "It was around nine this morning."

"Oh, my Lord! Did she tell you what happened?"

"She did. It was murder, Doctor."

"I thought as much. How is she?"

"Confused. At a loss. It's only natural. But Judy's doing better, now that she's with us."

"It's so tragic. But I'm calling mainly to warn you, Daniel, to get your family to safety. I'm certain Malcolm Claridge is behind this."

"Of the Claridge Foundation?"

"Yes, honestly, it's all my fault. Like an idiot, I wrote a detailed report of our meeting at your home—strictly for my professional colleagues, of course. Claridge intercepted it, and wanted a personal briefing. He's keenly interested in your device. What rich old man wouldn't be?"

"Don't blame yourself, Joseph. I halfway expected some sort of backlash after our talk, but I never figured an innocent young woman might lose her life. This subject is a very hot button. After this, things can only get worse. We're in uncharted territory now."

"Sadly, you're so right, Daniel. I think Claridge is capable of anything to get what he wants. He's had several bouts with cancer in recent years, and now you've provided the answer to his dreams—the ability to control his wealth and advance his agenda from beyond the grave. You must act immediately, Daniel. It might already be too late."

"You mean regarding Sarah and Jessica?"

"Yes, and Jerry Sterling too. You stand in the way of Claridge getting what he wants—control of your technology, for himself."

"You're right. We'll get right on it."

"Good luck, Daniel. Sorry I've been such a fool."

"Don't blame yourself, Joseph. Something had to happen. Let's talk again soon." Dan hung up.

Sarah was in tears. "Can Claridge get away with this?"

"I guess we'll see. But I know one thing—in the next five minutes, I'd like to see you grab some clothes and get your sweet self on the interstate to pick up Jessica."

"Okay."

Dan said, "Then, I think it'd make good sense for you to take her to your friend Janis' new place up that way."

"Great idea."

"But be careful. I'll let Jessica know you're coming."

Within minutes, Sarah was on her way north on the interstate.

Chapter 6

Jessica was third in a group of twelve girls hiking in the mountains with their camp counselors, when she saw her father. He was just ahead of the little troop, leaning against a tree and grinning. She waved to him discreetly, with her fingers, and stepped aside to let the other girls pass.

The leading camp counselor called back to her, "Let's keep up the pace, Jessica. We only have two more miles until lunch, back at camp."

The last of the group passed her. Jessica knelt down, as if she were having trouble with her shoe. "I'll catch up in a minute, Miss Nelson. I've got a rock in my shoe."

"A rock, huh?" said her father, smiling.

"Well, not really. Hi, Daddy."

"Hi, sweet pea."

Jessica continued the charade for her counselors by sitting down and removing her shoe.

"You're here about Mrs. Raymond, aren't you, Daddy?"

"That's right, honey. I figured you already knew. Smarty pants! Your mom is on her way up here to get you. Can you be ready in an hour?"

"Sure. We'll be back at camp soon."

"Thanks, honey. I'll check on you later." Dan waved.

Jessica waved back. "Bye, Daddy."

Her father disappeared. Jessica tied her shoe and ran to catch up.

Sarah had made good progress. She had just turned their SUV onto a gravel road a few miles from Jessica's summer camp. Two men in forest service uniforms—Carver and his partner, Bandini, a short muscular man—approached her car. Sarah stopped.

Carver stepped up to her raised driver's side window. "Sorry, ma'am. The road's out ahead."

Sarah lowered her window and said, "Is there another way around? I've got to..."

Carver reached inside and opened her door.

Sarah screamed, "No! No! Leave me alone!"

She scrambled toward the passenger door, but Bandini was waiting for her. Carver jumped in after her. Sarah kicked at him, landing a solid blow to his face. He yelled in pain and retreated.

Bandini broke the passenger window with the butt of his pistol and grabbed one of her wrists. Carver brutally dragged the screaming Sarah from the car. With a thud, her head struck the door's threshold, then the ground. Sarah fell silent and went limp.

No one was home. The Dutton vidphone rang ten times and started recording. The video image was blocked, and there was no caller ID. It was a man's voice. "Dutton. I have some bad news for you, man. We have your wife. Her pretty face is a little bruised, but otherwise I think she's okay. Maybe not. I can't ask her—she's unconscious at the moment. Either way, she is kinda hot. If you wanna see the bitch alive again, you'll lay off saying another word about your work. Oh, I almost forgot...your daughter's next. Have a nice day."

That evening, the Dutton doorbell rang. The electric lock clicked open and Joseph Smithson stepped inside. He entered the living room. Dan was there. From the speaker, Dan said, "Thanks for coming, Joseph."

Jerry entered from the kitchen with a beer in his hand. "Hey, Doc, have a beer." He handed Smithson the bottle and went back for another.

"Thank you, Jerry, that looks great just now. Have you heard anything from Sarah?" Joseph took a long swig of his beer.

"More or less," said Dan. "One of Claridge's goons left a message." He played it back for Smithson.

"Christ!" said Joseph. "I was afraid something like this would happen."

Jerry was back with his beer.

Outside, Carver and Bandini rolled to a quiet stop. They noticed Smithson's car in the driveway. Bandini elbowed Carver and said, "The old man was right."

Back inside the house, Smithson asked, "What about Jessica?"

Dan said, "I screwed up and sent Sarah off without a device on her phone. Fortunately, the camp director was able to convince Claridge's men that Jerry had already picked Jessica up, which he did—an hour later. I'd called the camp earlier and given them fair warning, just in case."

"Well," said Joseph, "at least the child is safe."

"She's at a friend's." After a long silence, Dan asked, "Joseph, what do you think would happen if we called in the authorities?"

"Oh, my Lord! With Claridge behind this, Sarah would most certainly be killed."

"Then we'll have to go public."

"Public? I thought that was only an option if nothing went wrong."

Dan said, "I'm not going to be inflexible when Sarah's life is at stake. We free her first, then we go public."

"But how on earth do we find her?"

"It's not possible for them to hide Sarah from me. She's safe, for the moment, in a sub-basement of the university hospital, near the morgue."

Jerry took a swig of his beer and added, "Show him Judy's drawing."

"Drawing?" asked Smithson.

"Yeah," said Jerry, "Judy left Sarah a drawing."

Dan told Smithson what had happened to Sarah's phone and shared a photo of the flower drawing. "It was Judy's way of saying hi."

"Oh my, will wonders never cease? Who'd have thought such a thing was possible?"

Dan said, "My thoughts exactly. But first things first. Hey, Jer."

Jerry was just downing his last swig. "Huh?"

"Do we know anyone who might be interested in volunteering for a special mission tonight? Maybe after another beer?"

Jerry's eyes opened wide when he asked, "What was that you said about a morgue?"

Chapter 7

An ambulance pulled up to the hospital's service entrance. Jerry hopped out wearing an EMT's uniform. He pulled a gurney out of the back and slammed the door. An interface foxtail was dangling from his shirt pocket. He unlocked the service door, with a key furnished by the good doctor, dragged the gurney inside, and pushed it to a nearby service elevator. He poked a finger at the down button.

Carver and Bandini were in their car outside the employee exit. A big man in an orderly's uniform left the building and headed for the parking lot. Carver elbowed his partner and said, "There he is."

Half asleep, Bandini came around and looked at his watch. "About time, he's two hours late."

Now inside the elevator, Jerry watched the numbers on the display as it descended—B...SB1...SB2...SB3. "Okay, we're here." The elevator door opened and Jerry wheeled out the gurney. Lighting was minimal, but a sign indicated that the morgue, autopsy rooms, and cadaver vault were ahead. "Geez! This is terrific, Dan. Doctor Frankenstein would love this place."

From the fox-tailed phone in Jerry's pocket Dan said, "I'll trade with you, Jerry. You should see what it looks like from my side."

From Dan's point of view, they weren't alone. A menacing apparition of a long-dead corpse was screaming in their faces in an effort to frighten them off. Jerry looked right through it, totally oblivious of its presence. "No, thanks," said Jerry. This place is creepy enough just the way it is."

Long-dead addressed Dan, "Oh, it's you again. Brought some help this time, huh?" Inches from Jerry's face, he said, "I don't think your deputy here is quite up to handling the hoods who brought her down here. Those are some really bad boys—and they're coming back."

Dan said, "Really? Thanks."

"For what?" asked Jerry.

"Sorry, Jer, there's someone else here. I'll be back in a few minutes. We have company coming."

Dan moved to the parking lot, where he found Carver and Bandini walking toward the emergency entrance. Then he moved again—this time to an elevator shed on the hospital's roof. There he entered the structure and reached into a big circuit box, bending one particular relay's contact arm.

Jerry decided to check things out up ahead. He arrived at the cadaver vault first. The sign on the vault door had been crossed out. The correction read, "Senior Professor's Lounge." Jerry grinned. He opened the door and a pungent fog enveloped him. Corpses on gurneys lined the walls. He stepped inside and shivered as he approached a huge waist-high vat. Its surface was obscured by a thick acrid chemical fog. He waved the mist away with his hands, exposing two floating cadavers whose glazed eyes stared up at him as they bobbed in the vat's preservative. He waved a second time and a dozen more cadavers were exposed. He said, "Geez Louise, what a lovely place."

Carver and Bandini passed through the busy emergency room area, dressed as orderlies. "Damn," said Bandini. "Hold on a second, man."

Carver stopped in his tracks. "What?"

"I hadn't noticed 'til just now. But damn, that's one helluva black eye she gave you."

"Well, screw you too, man! Let's just stop the foolin' around and do what we came here for."

"Okay, okay, but it's still the best shiner I've ever seen."

They stepped up to the same service elevator Jerry had used earlier. Carver hit the down button with his fist.

Up in the rooftop elevator shed, a relay clicked. Its bent contact arm moved, but failed to make contact.

Carver and Bandini waited.

Bandini said, "What's the deal with the broad?"

"Hell, if I know. I just do what I'm told. The old man wanted her dumped in the cadaver vat if Smithson showed up at the Dutton place. Smithson's next."

"Helluva way to go."

In Sub-basement Three, Dan arrived where he'd left Jerry, who was nowhere to be seen.

Long-dead rushed up. "Told you so, didn't I?"

"Thanks for the warning."

Dan looked toward the cadaver vault and saw Jerry's gurney in the corridor. There were countless disembodied about, a virtual log jam. He made his way past them and through the closed vault door. "Hey, Jer. I thought you might be exploring."

Jerry jumped. "Christ, Dan! You scared the crap outta me."

"Sorry, Jer. We've got company coming. I think I slowed them down a little."

They exited the vault. Jerry pushed the gurney to Autopsy One and stuck his head inside. An intern was hunched over a body on the table; he looked up.

Jerry said, "Hi, Doc."

"If you're looking for the morgue, it's two doors down."

"Thanks, Doc."

Back on the first floor and still waiting, Carver looked at his watch. "Damn it. Screw this! Let's find another way." There was no stairwell nearby, so they walked back toward the E.R.

In the sub-basement, outside Autopsy Two, Dan remarked, "Nobody's in there, Jerry. Sarah's in the room around the corner. She's been drugged, probably won't respond."

"I'll have her outta there in a jiffy."

They stopped where the halls intersected. An exit sign marked the door to the stairwell. Dan said, "I'll be back in a minute, Jer. Try not to let anyone through this door."

"You got it."

Dan disappeared.

Jerry turned and almost tripped over a stack of lumber piled up against the wall. He found Sarah's room and opened the door.

Up near the E.R., Carver was speaking with a janitor, who pointed toward a door just behind Bandini. Carver handed the man several bills and returned. "Fuckin' waste of time!" They entered the stairwell.

In Sarah's room, Jerry shoved the gurney length-wise up against the near side of her hospital bed. Sarah appeared to be unconscious. Her left temple was bruised and bloodied, but had stopped bleeding; there was dried blood on her blouse and the bed linen. Jerry didn't want to startle her, so he whispered, "Sarah, I'm going to pull you onto this gurney." She didn't respond. Jerry reached across the gurney, grabbed her clothing, and pulled her to him. He then covered Sarah with a sheet, up to her shoulders, and strapped her down. He left the room, parked the gurney around the corner, and then started rummaging through the stack of 2x4s in the hallway.

Carver and Bandini passed Dan on the second landing. Dan reached into a light fixture on the wall—the lights flickered and went out.
Carver looked around and said, "Shit, no emergency lights!"
In the dark, Bandini tripped and fell down the stairs. "Owww! Son-of-a-bitch!"
"Hey," said Carver. "There's a light on a few levels down."
"Damn it!" yelled Bandini, "Thanks for that newsy tidbit. But kiss my ass, I just banged the fuck outta my knee!"

Jerry had selected a board long enough to reach the valve in the insulated steam pipe above him. He positioned the board's end against the valve and shoved upward with all his strength. When the pipe broke, Jerry dropped the board, grabbed the gurney, and raced toward the elevator. Scalding steam filled the corridor, blasting the stairwell door.
The intern in Autopsy One stuck his head out and called, "What happened?"
Looking back and yelling over his shoulder, Jerry replied, "Looks like you sprung a leak, Doc."
Dan was back. "Great idea, Jerry!"
Jerry reached the elevator and poked a finger at the button. Nothing happened.
Dan said, "Oops! Wait a few seconds and try it again, Jer. I've gotta fix the elevator." Dan disappeared.
Sarah, dazed and groggy, opened her eyes and said, "Hi, Jerry."

Jerry smiled and said, "Hi, Sarah. You okay?"

"My head hurts. What's going on? Are those men gone?" She tried to raise her arm to touch her sore head.

Jerry hit the elevator button again.

"Sorry, hon. I've got you strapped down. We're almost outta here. I'm gonna take you somewhere where a doctor can fix you up. Hang on tight. We're in a bit of a rush." The elevator door opened.

Carver and Bandini reached the bottom of the stairs, where an emergency light was on. Steam blasted the outside of the exit window. Carver yelled at Bandini, "Open it!"

Bandini yelled back, "You open it, asshole! I'm not that stupid." Carver pushed the door open, and screamed in pain. Bandini smiled. "What'd I say, wise guy?"

Outside, Jerry shoved the gurney into the back of the ambulance, climbed inside, and slammed the doors behind him. He freed Sarah's arms, but otherwise left her strapped down. He said, "It's okay now, Sarah. No one's going to hurt you."

Sarah, still groggy, smiled and said, "Bless you, Jerry."

Jerry jumped behind the wheel and started the engine. Dan jumped through the right door and landed in the passenger seat. He grinned and said, "Great rescue, Jerry!" Jerry punched the accelerator.

The tires squealed as the ambulance sped away.

Chapter 8

Later that morning, Carver was being grilled by Claridge. "What do you mean, you couldn't get to the room? So the Dutton woman is still alive!"

Looking like he had a very bad sunburn, Carver replied, "It's true, sir. We wound up waiting most of the night for the morgue orderly to leave—turns out it was the day guy I'd paid to look the other way."

"Good thinking." Claridge grimaced and held a hand to his chest. He reached for a nearby bottle of pills, popped two into his mouth, and followed them with a long swig of water. "You idiots will be the death of me yet."

Carver continued, "We were on our way down to finish her off, when we ran into a big steam leak. The elevator wasn't working, and now the place is crawling with cops."

"Doesn't that sound suspicious to you?"

"I suppose so, sir."

"So the Dutton woman is still down by the morgue?"

"As far as I know."

Claridge grabbed a heavy bronze paperweight from his desk and threw it at Carver. Carver dodged it. It bounced off the heavy oak door with a thud.

"Don't screw with me, Carver. You and that half-witted partner of yours have one more chance. One more. If you can't get me Dutton's wife, get me his daughter. Today!"

"But, sir, we went to the kid's camp in the mountains, just after we nabbed her mother. She's gone."

"I don't care what you've tried. I want that child today! Now get out of my face."

Carver quickly exited through the library door.

Claridge picked up the phone and began dialing. His intercom signaled. He slammed the phone down and jabbed a finger at the intercom. "What is it?"

"It's Bill Spellman, sir. He says he's here to see you on urgent business."

"Well, damn it, send him in!"

Spellman, Claridge's attorney, entered on a run. The man was breathless and red-faced. He looked around the room anxiously and finally grabbed the remote for the big-screen television across the room.

"What are you up to, Spellman? Have you lost your mind?"

Spellman was frantically working the buttons on the remote. "Here, excuse me, Malcolm. You've got to see this!"

On the television, a familiar male TV personality was in mid-interview. "Are there plans to release this technology to the public?"

Joseph Smithson's visage filled the screen. He said, "Dutton plans to make the device available to the public later this year. Any attempt to control its use will result in the automatic dissemination of the technology, from a hundred worldwide repositories simultaneously."

"Why is it, Doctor, that it has been decided to go public with these facts at this particular time?"

"Because an innocent young woman was murdered to obtain her silence regarding this affair. The death is under investigation. Authorities are also investigating a second crime, the abduction and conspiracy to murder Dutton's wife, Sarah. Sarah, I'm happy to say, was spirited out of captivity early this morning."

There was a thunderous crash. Spellman spun around to find that his employer had fallen out of his chair.

"Ow!" howled Claridge. "Don't just stand there, Spellman. Call Doctor Sparks! I need him here immediately."

"Certainly, sir."

Grimacing in pain, Claridge roared, "So Dutton's wife was spirited out of captivity early this morning? I've had enough! Find Carver and Bandini. I want them out of the picture. Ow! Those amateurs will be the end of me yet."

Spellman fumbled for his cell phone.

"And Spellman, call Leonard Palkin at the institute. He should have been involved in this from the beginning. Now there'll be hell to pay."

Later that afternoon, Carver and Bandini exited a fast food restaurant and approached their car, parked behind the establishment. Bandini was still limping. Just as they reached their vehicle, a van skidded to a stop behind them. Three armed men jumped out. Bandini produced his pistol and managed to get off a single, poorly-aimed shot before the weapon was brutally kicked out of his hand. Carver had no stomach for it, and willingly surrendered his weapon. They were roughly shoved into the van at gunpoint and it sped away.

An hour later, the van pulled off a highway onto a gravel road. A cloud of dust followed as the vehicle tracked an abandoned rail spur out of sight and behind a sandstone outcropping. The van stopped abruptly and the sliding side door opened. Without a word, Carver and Bandini, gagged and with their hands bound behind their backs, were roughly shoved out to the ground. Their captors jumped out behind them. As the captives struggled to get to their feet, they were each shot in the head. Their bodies were left where they'd fallen. The van sped away in a cloud of dust.

Sarah's head was bandaged. Jerry exclaimed, "Jesus Christ, look at this." Jerry, Sarah, and Jessica had arrived at the Dutton residence to find that the neighborhood had become a parking lot.

Media vehicles all but blocked the street. A throng of media and onlookers covered their lawn. The police had a barricade blocking the Duttons' driveway.

Jerry drove his BMW up to the barricade. A policeman signaled him to stop. Jerry rolled down his window and the officer said, "I'm sorry, sir, but you'll have to park somewhere else."

Sarah said, "I don't think you understand, officer. I'm Sarah Dutton. This is my home. Can't you do something about this crowd?"

The officer motioned for one of his colleagues to move the barricade aside. "I'm sorry, ma'am. As far as the crowd goes—well, ma'am, you folks are big news."

Jerry parked the car while several police officers parted the noisy crowd, clearing a route to the front door. Sarah held Jessica firmly by the hand as they exited the vehicle and headed toward the house. A barrage of questions ensued.

"Mrs. Dutton, will your husband be making himself available for an interview soon?"

"Mrs. Dutton, are you aware that the Reverend Alvin Sheets has damned you and your family as blasphemers?"

"Mrs. Dutton, will licensing agreements for your husband's device be granted soon?"

"Now that we can talk with the dead, will your husband be helping the authorities locate those responsible for the thousands of unsolved murders?"

"Is it true that Mr. Dutton and Elvis are close friends? Will Elvis be granting an interview this evening?"

As they approached the porch, Jerry spoke into Sarah's ear, "I'll deal with them, Sarah. You should rest."

"Let me try, Jerry."

When they finally reached the porch, Sarah turned to the crowd and said, "I'm certain that Daniel will want to make himself available for an interview, but not like this. I suggest you put your heads together and pick one single individual to interview my husband—one reporter from the legitimate press to be his contact, just one. You people working for the scandal sheets and their equivalent in the broadcast media, I suggest that you take a hike and go out and get a real job."

The crowd laughed.

That night, a network television truck—satellite antenna and all—was parked in the Dutton driveway. The police were still dealing with a boisterous crowd of media and onlookers.

The television crew had set up in the living room. A dozen cables snaked out toward the kitchen door. Marsha Gambles, a well-known network interviewer, had just begun her interview with Daniel Dutton. Joseph Smithson and Jerry were seated on the sofa. Dan stood nearby. Sarah and Jessica were watching from the kitchen doorway.

Marsha was saying, "I don't know where to begin, Mr. Dutton, so I'll just jump in. What's it like being dead?"

From the foxtail device on the coffee table, Dan responded, "I bet that's the first time you've asked that question in an interview. Well—it's different. It's not unpleasant. In fact, I haven't felt this good since I was a child."

Marsha said, "Excuse me, but it's hard for me to actually believe any of this. It's hard to believe this isn't a put-on. Why should we believe this, Mr. Dutton?"

"Because it's true. It's probably the most important truth of all."

"That you're talking with us from the dead?"

"No, that's not quite what I meant. The important fact here is that the death of our bodies is not the end of us. It's quite an experience to abruptly find yourself so unwittingly immortal."

"Why should we believe this? Couldn't this be a prank at our expense?"

"It could be a hoax, but it's not. What would it take to convince you that I am the deceased Daniel Dutton?"

Marsha paused at some length and finally said, "That's really a difficult question. I don't know."

"I thought not. You can't use any conventional means to verify my identity. None of them still apply to someone without a body. So what remains?"

"I don't know."

"I'll tell you—I remain. The essence of Daniel Dutton remains—the spirit, the memory, the personality. Only the physical attributes are absent. Only to others am I different."

"What do you miss?"

"I miss eating—strangely, I still get hungry. I miss physical intimacy."

The deceased Marla Culpepper, in her nightgown, walked from the kitchen holding her disembodied cat and sat on the sofa between Joseph and Jerry. She raised the cat's paw and waved it at the camera.

Marsha went on, "Back to the problem of your identity, Daniel. How can that be proven?"

"Well, Marsha, I guess it's up to you, and the others hung up on that point, to decide. Maybe you could ask people who know me."

"What about those in the scientific community?"

"What about them?"

"How are you going to prove this to them?"

"I'm not. The proof of any innovation is whether or not it works. Way back when, it was common knowledge that the world was flat. Until someone actually checked it out."

Marsha paused a moment and said, "I guess you're right. It shouldn't make any difference."

"There are no authorities on this subject, none living anyway. So it's up to a dead man to tell the tale, and to tell the tale, one has to have a voice."

"I know you're right, Daniel. Are you aware of other spirits with us?"

"There are two here with us right now. But there are many, many others."

Marsha's eyes widened and she asked, "Others? There are other spirits here with us? Why have they come to you?"

"Actually, one of them was here when we moved in, years ago. She and her cat."

"This house was haunted when you moved in?"

"In a manner of speaking. She helped me perfect the device I'm using. The second person was one we knew before her death." Judy Raymond had appeared beside Sarah and Jessica at the kitchen door. "She came here, where there is hope. You can't know how sad, how stricken one feels at the abrupt and total loss of any hope of communication with the living."

"You and your device are her only hope for this sadness? I guess I've never thought about it. I guess I've never really been alone."

"Imagine," said Dan. "Imagine yourself suddenly shunned by everyone, even family and friends. Imagine yourself totally ignored. You see them, but they don't see you. Grasp that, and you'll have some appreciation for the mental state of the newly-deceased. It drives the disembodied to whatever means they have at hand. And so we have ghosts, and poltergeists and the like."

"But aren't you a ghost?"

"I would be if I were trying to reach out to the living, using whatever means I possessed, like ghostly images."

"Can you do such things?" asked Marsha.

"If you'd like."

Suddenly the room turned bitterly cold. Marsha shivered. A fog formed throughout the room and quickly migrated toward its center, right in front of the camera. The fog took on the form of a man, a man carved out of wispy, translucent marble. Marsha recognized the face from her research. It was Daniel Dutton. The features relaxed and came to life. The face winked and smiled.

From the image Dan asked, "How's this?"

Shivering and dumbfounded, Marsha exclaimed, "Oh my gosh, Daniel. Is that you? I never thought I'd see such a thing!" To her cameraman, she said, "I hope you're getting this, Barney. Tell me you're getting this."

Barney replied, "It's on the monitor, Mar. I just hope it's making it to memory."

Dan's image winked again, and suddenly disappeared. Immediately the room warmed up. The fog vanished.

Dan said, "Anything else?"

"Anything else?" exclaimed Marsha. "Oh, my Lord! Wow—that was fantastic! Well...let me think. Would it be possible to locate someone dead for several years?" (Marsha had someone particular in mind.)

"It's possible, though I can't say that it's likely. If I've known them, I can often find them easily enough—dead or alive. I think it's fairly unlikely that, after several years, any one individual might not have moved on—though a few do hang around for a very long while."

"What do you mean, *moved on*?"

"Let me put it this way," said Dan. "Several places where you're certain to find the disembodied in significant numbers are maternity wards, delivery rooms, and in proximity to pregnant women in their third trimester."

Chapter 9

Jerry Sterling threaded his way through a tangle of students in the hallway outside the office of Gil Raymond, biology instructor and fencing coach at Stellington Junior College. He waited as Raymond finished a discussion with one of his students, a cute little blonde of eighteen or so. Raymond was smiling.

Gil was some fifteen years older than his young wife had been. He wore a tight-fitting black knit shirt that accentuated his muscular physique. Gil noticed Jerry through his open door—as the girl left, he waved him in. "What can I do for you?"

"Gilbert Raymond?"

"That's me."

Jerry offered his hand and Gil shook it firmly. "Mr. Raymond, I'm Jerry Sterling. I'm an attorney representing Daniel and Sarah Dutton. I wonder if I might speak with you for a few minutes."

"Glad to meet you, Counselor." Gil's smile had vanished.

"Mind if I take a seat and set this down?" Jerry raised the briefcase he was carrying.

"Suit yourself." Gil indicated a nearby chair and closed the door. He returned to his seat and asked, "Is this official business, Counselor? I just buried my wife yesterday, I could use a short break before something else goes wrong."

Jerry sat down and placed his briefcase on the floor. "It's nothing like that, Mr. Raymond. I'm not here in my capacity as legal counsel, but more as a personal representative."

"Good." Gil paused a moment, then said, "Dutton. Dutton? Is that the 'Daniel Dutton' Marsha Gambles interviewed?"

"It is."

"I streamed it a few days ago, and the interview with Smithson. Don't know that I can swallow all that. Good special effects though. I'm an old fan of Dutton's—but I think maybe people are taking *this* science fiction a bit too seriously."

"I guess we'll have to wait and see."

"Maybe so. Speaking of Smithson, he was treating my wife. I thought he seemed pretty level-headed—until that interview."

Jerry could see this wasn't going to be easy. "Maybe I should get to the point."

"Maybe so."

"I told you I represent the Duttons. Well, I also represent another individual, whom you know personally."

"And who is that?"

"Judith Megan Raymond—your wife."

Gil jumped to his feet. "What the hell—what are you up to? Oh, I get it now! You represent Daniel Dutton, so you're trying to say my wife is one of those spirits. The ones he claimed were with him during the interview. You're here to give me a message from my dead wife, like the ones Dutton's been passing out to other relatives of the dead."

"You're partly right, Judy was one of the individuals he mentioned in the Gambles interview."

"Okay, lay it on me—what's the message?"

"What I have is not a message, as such. What I have is a communication link."

"A link. Like Dutton's?"

"That's correct. I have it here with me." Jerry lifted his briefcase.

"You're saying I'll be able to talk with my wife?"

"That's right."

"Right now?"

"That's up to you."

"Hey, you're *really* serious!"

"If I were in your place, I'd take it home with me. It might be best where you won't be disturbed."

"All...all right," agreed Raymond.

"Good. I have the link and instructions in this briefcase—along with one of my business cards. Call me, when it's convenient."

Gil decided to wait until that evening. He hated coming home. It just reminded him of Judy.

The handwritten instructions were simple enough—as was the link—a smartphone with a foxtail. Somehow he had figured it'd be much more complicated. He turned on the phone and tapped an icon. Nothing happened. So he reread the instructions. The last item was *Say something*. So he said, "What do you want me to say?"

"How you've been doing, Gil." It was unmistakably Judy's voice, but somehow different.

Gil's hair stood on end. A chill passed through his body. He jumped to his feet and quickly crossed the room. His eyes filled with tears. "Judy, honey. Is that you?"

"It's me, Gil, sweetheart. It's me."

"I can't believe it! This can't be happening, it just can't be happening!"

"It is, sweetheart. Believe it. It is me. It's a miracle, I know, but it's real."

Gil paced the floor. The tears flowed so heavily, he couldn't see. He wiped them away with the back of his hand, but they kept coming. "This has to be a trick, a cruel trick."

"Listen to me, Gil. It's not a trick. It's not a trick. It's what Daniel Dutton was talking about. I know you've seen it. That's what you told Jerry Sterling this afternoon."

"How can something like this happen?"

"It happened when a dedicated man single-handedly bucked all the reasons why he couldn't do something wonderful, and did it anyway."

"But what does it mean?"

"It means that death can't keep us apart, sweetheart. It means we can still be together. We can still experience things together, we can still...we can still live together."

Gil stopped in his tracks, dumbstruck. "How? What do you mean?"

"Like Dan and Sarah Dutton. They still live together."

Gil covered his eyes with his hands and turned away. "This is too much for me all at once. First, you're dead. I saw your dead body, Judy. I touched you. You were cold as ice. Jesus! I buried you yesterday! Now you want to live with me—as a ghost?"

Judy responded, "I'm sorry, Gil. I'd hoped..."

Gil's tears were gone. "Are you going to do something like the show Dutton put on for the media? Christ, Judy, this gives me the creeps. This is just too much, too fast. I can't keep up. I don't believe this. I can't believe this!"

"Okay, Gil. I understand; I'll leave you alone. I doubted you still wanted me when you were mean the other night, when you laughed at me again. And then tried to have me committed. I just wanted to make sure. Now I know. Anyway—if you want to talk, I'll be around." Judy released the interface and was gone.

She went back to Dan and Sarah's, but she kept a ghostly little finger on Gil's interface, just in case he decided he wanted to talk.

Judy and Sarah had become great friends in the few days since she'd learned to use the device.

Jerry and Dan had been talking about moving all of them to a place in the mountains. A place where they'd be less vulnerable to the mob that hung about their city home.

Judy liked the term *disembodied* better than *dead*—that term had little meaning to her now. If you were talking about meat or door nails, it applied—but if you were talking about people, people who could still have relationships, it meant little.

As one of the disembodied for a week now, Judy really couldn't complain. She felt the same, actually better. She was with people who cared about her, who loved her. And she had hope for the future. What else could she ask for? Well, maybe that Gil would want her back. But it seemed unlikely. He'd been very mean after her visit with Sarah Dutton, so mean she'd had her breakdown. At least she had a future now, and she was part of something that could change the world—change it for the better. Something she was certain would change the world like nothing else.

Gil made no effort to speak with Judy in the days following their encounter. Even so, she checked on him most evenings. Certainly he once felt affection for her, but it would never be the same. They'd grown apart in many ways, especially since they'd lost Penny. She knew Gil, he was very much driven by physical needs—he had no need for her now.

Judy sensed little of herself in his thoughts. In her place his attention drifted repeatedly to another woman—a living, breathing woman he could get his hands on—one, she sensed, he'd known before her death. The night Gil slept with the woman, Judy made herself absent.

After the broadcast with Smithson, Ernest Feemish decided it might be wise to make himself disappear. If Claridge were furious with Smithson, he'd be getting around to Feemish soon enough. After all, Feemish had learned about the Dutton affair from Smithson's report, just as Claridge had. So, Ernest quickly arranged to take an extended vacation; his wife had a sister in Utah. With the cat in its carrier and a trunk full of luggage, they attempted an all-night run to Salt Lake.

They'd just had a meal at a roadside diner and were back on the highway. Ernest was driving. He exclaimed, "Damn! I let us leave without the audio book drive on the mantel. Maybe we can find something to listen to on the radio."

Just then the car jumped, something had hit them from behind. Panicking, Ernest almost lost control. He looked in the rearview mirror—there were headlights nearly on top of them. He quickly looked over his shoulder. "Oh, my Lord! There's a van right on our bumper! I think it rammed us." The van rammed them again, and backed off.

Irene lost it. She shrieked, and yelled, "What do they want, Ernest? Oh, Jesus, what do we do?" Then she just screamed.

"Will you please shut up, Irene? It's all I can do just to keep us on the road!"

A little ahead of them a sign read *Eagle Canyon*. Beyond the sign the highway began a curve, followed by a bridge over the canyon.

They passed the sign and were nearing the curve, when the van came full-bore against their rear bumper. It forced them off the road and toward the canyon edge.

Ernest fought the steering wheel to regain some directional control and avoid the inevitable.

The van rapidly accelerated and then suddenly—stopped.

Ernest hit the brakes with all his might, but it was too late. Their car slowed, but couldn't stop. It slipped over the canyon edge, and was gone. All that remained was the cloud of dust in the van's headlights.

Without formal instruction, the interface wasn't difficult to figure out. The foxtail functioned much like the brain's speech-control circuitry, except that an articulation-processor and speaker supplanted the physical human voice mechanisms.

And so, once the device became public knowledge, the dead began trying their hand at it.

The first time it happened, Sarah had been home alone. It had been a man's voice. Sarah never understood how the device discerned what gender a decedent had been, even after Dan had explained it. As it turned out, it was someone they knew, a physician who had worked with Dan's father.

It wasn't long before there was essentially a ghostly riot over control of Dutton's device.

"Oh, Lord, please save me…"

Mr. Dutton, please help me—I was…"

"Where's my mommy? Please help me find my mommy…"

"Hey, Dutton, this is Tom Weese, your old Army buddy. How about a hand, man?"

"If I could scream through this thing, I would…"

"This 'dead shit' really sucks, but it beats what I'd been expecting. If you decide to run for President, you got my vote."

"Where do I go to get one of these?"

"I've been waiting years for Jesus and saw your…"

"Hey, Dutton, who's in charge here? Helluva way to run an afterlife. No pearly gates. No light at the end of the tunnel. No Jesus. Only good thing about this is—I'm not in Hell. And then there's this alone bit."

Sarah freaked out and took Jessica to a friend's place until Dan added something akin to password protection to the program and finally regained control.

Late one night, Terra heard something behind the house. She didn't bark, but went down to the patio door, tapped the glass with her paw, and the dog latch (another of Daniel's innovations) slid the door open. There was a full moon. The collie crept out the door and silently made her way toward the back fence, near the zinnias, where Sarah's waterfall gurgled day and night.

There, Terra found two men. One was on his back. Ned, their Garden Guardian, was standing on the man's chest with his laser weapon poised and ready.

The second man was stuck on the fence. The assault weapon he'd carried across his back, where the sling crossed his chest, had become caught on one of the pickets of the tall fence as he was climbing over. His pants, weighed down by pounds of assault gear attached to his belt, were down about his ankles. There, too, Ned was the responsible party.

Terra joined in on the fun and tugged at the trousers of the man on the fence. She barked for help. When the authorities arrived, the intruders were deprived of their weapons, handcuffed, and hauled away. It all fell within Ned's mission of keeping pests and vermin out of the yard and away from the house.

Chapter 10

Evangelist Alvin Sheets was on a stage behind dozens of microphones. Below him scores of media types were hanging on his every word. "This heresy is a crime against God! I beg all my followers, and all good Christians everywhere, to contribute to our war chest. And in so doing, to contribute to the fight against these children of Satan assembling to damn and corrupt the souls of our dear departed."

Somewhere in the Deep South, the Grand Dragon addressed a lone cameraman and a crowd of yelling, wild-eyed Klansmen. "Now git this straight. There ain't no way that no soulless minorities will evah be commin' back as white men in no next life. Not while I'm Grand Dragon."

At a Buddhist temple in Chennai, India, a Buddhist priest addressed an Eastern reporter and camera crew. "I am so pleased that finally the Western World is being blessed with the opportunity to appreciate the true nature of Man. This is a precious gift, a chance for the West to break away from the materialism and body-worship of its mortal view of existence." He bowed, with his hands in prayer, "Oh, yes, I am so pleased."

Marsha Gambles was in a television studio addressing the broadcast audience of her national Sunday news magazine. "And things are indeed happening following our interview with the deceased Daniel Dutton just a month ago."

A video clip was playing—showing an auditorium, where organization officers on a stage were responding to a vote just taken by the assembled members. Marsha said, "In Boston, a national psychiatric group—of which Dr. Joseph Smithson, one of Dutton's supporters, has been a career-long member—voted today to expel the good doctor from its membership. Its spokesperson later attacked Smithson and Dutton as "Charlatans out to delude an impressionable public."

A clip of a stately Paris mansion aired as Marsha reported. "In Paris yesterday, a spokesman for legendary finance guru Vincent Alfors, reputedly on his deathbed following a protracted illness, made an admission. His employer, Alfors, had offered Dutton millions if Dutton would provide him with an interface immediately. Dutton's response to Alfors isn't known.

"Here in the U.S., many messages to be forwarded to the dead have been received 'in care-of the Duttons'. An e-mail address dedicated to this purpose is shown here on your viewing screen. As a result, the gymnasium at Wexler Canyon Junior College, near Albuquerque, has had its walls put to good use—as a bulletin board to the dead. Messages to dead, or *late*, recipients are posted alphabetically from ceiling to floor, already covering over half the available wall space." A video showed a cherry picker being used to post the messages.

"From Rodeo Drive, in Beverly Hills, comes a tale from renowned psychic and medium Melanie Anguish." A video clip displayed the psychic's Rodeo Drive storefront. "According to Melanie, she was in the middle of a seance for a very exclusive group, when an alien calling himself Boolong of Korgrill appeared as an apparition. Melanie claimed that Boolong pleaded with her to enlist Daniel Dutton 'to recruit souls for the thousands of soulless bodies roaming his planet as zombies.'"

"On a more serious note—or maybe not—in Albuquerque last night, two apparently religiously-motivated armed men, each claiming to be acting alone, which seems very unlikely, were apprehended by authorities in the Dutton's back yard. The two had been immobilized and placed under citizen's arrest by the Dutton's collie, Terra, and their little Garden Guardian robot, unquestionably the most ubiquitous of Dutton's creations.

"Perhaps the most interesting turn of events is that the dead were watching my interview with Daniel Dutton. At least several of them are now using what Dutton calls a *Scratchpad Interface*. There are only two so far. The prototype has been placed on loan to one of the local libraries, in a locked room. The system uses a tablet computer and an app, again created by Dutton, making the writing of handwritten messages easily accessible to the dead. An interesting aspect of this particular innovation is, as Dutton has noted, that one might substantiate a decedent's identity by examining his or her handwriting.

"We'll share a few of the messages with you." On the screen behind Marsha appeared a woman's photo. "Bernice Spelling, of Topeka, dead for a week now, maintains that her funeral was a farce and that her husband, Fred, who is now living with a young woman less than half his age—'Did it on purpose.'

"And here's another—a most interesting statement from one Aaron Bransom of San Francisco. Mr. Bransom claims that he was murdered last December by his wife and her lover, for several very large life insurance benefits. The clincher is, that Mr. Bransom claims to know the whereabouts of certain physical evidence proving their guilt. He has requested that his message be forwarded to the authorities and to the insurance companies in question.

"I spoke with Jacob Michaels this morning, president of one of the insurance companies impacted, Norrington Life, of Hartford, Connecticut. Here is his response via video call:

"Are you kidding? We'd love to have proof that claimants murdered our insured. What an innovation! Now when a death is involved, all the police and insurance adjusters have to do is ask the deceased. I can't wait until the dead are being called to the witness stand. So much for murdering someone to silence them as a witness!"

"And finally, a fantastic story from Oslo, confirmed by a reliable source in Washington." A video of peace negotiations in Oslo was screened behind Marsha. "It seems that Dutton's technology has been instrumental in peace negotiations that were cut short by the untimely death of America's U.N. Ambassador, Millard Sherman. Ambassador Sherman died of a heart attack in Oslo last Saturday. We are told today that the ambassador himself has been making use of a Dutton device since his demise.

"While Ambassador Sherman's untimely death may have slowed crucial negotiations, it has also provided a solution. The parties have, just this afternoon, agreed to a peace proposal offered by the deceased Ambassador Sherman."

Chapter 11

Three weeks later, outside the White House, a limo approached the gate through a crowd of picketers. Their signs read along the lines of, "Outlaw Dutton's Device, Save Our Dearly Departed," and "To Hell with Dutton." A few moments later, Senator William Brighton exited the limo and entered the building.

Soon after, in the Oval Office, President Theodore Forester was seated in an armchair. Senator Brighton, Secretary of State Robert Cannon, and F.B.I. Director Charles Simmons were seated nearby. President Forester, nodding in the direction of the protestors, asked, "What do you gentlemen make of the commotion Daniel Dutton has stirred up?"

Brighton took the lead, "I can tell you, Mr. President, that's all they're talking about back home, even here in Washington. If you can't support Dutton, I suggest that you *at* least have no *official* opinion."

"I see," said President Forester, nodding.

"If one of your people as much as jokes about this, you might as well resign yourself to sitting out a single term in the White House latrine. Believe me, Alvin Sheets orchestrated this demonstration; it has absolutely nothing to do with American public opinion. Look at it this way—if you were Joe Public, and someone just handed you proof of your own immortality and then provided you with the means to maintain relationships, control property, and pursue your personal goals from beyond the grave —you'd be ecstatic."

"Certainly," said Forester, "if I were convinced of the truth of it."

"Believe me, Ted, most Americans are convinced it's true, and so am I. I've spoken with Dutton at length. This is for real. The point is, if you were among the thousands who know the truth of this, and you'd received a message from your dead child or spouse, and Uncle Sam showed up to tax or regulate the device that made that possible—why, you'd tell the son-of-a-bitch to go right to hell. And the people in power wouldn't be in power very long. It would be easier for us to regulate religion."

Secretary Cannon added, "I agree with Bill. Regardless of race or faith, our world is spellbound by these events."

Forester said, "I don't imagine Ambassador Sherman's message hurt."

"It was electrifying!" said Cannon. "It has been suggested that you should reinstate Sherman as Ambassador."

Wide-eyed, Forester said, "Really?" He turned to Director Simmons, "And what does the Bureau know of all this, Charlie?"

"Quite a bit, Mr. President. For starters, it doesn't look like the Duttons made any money off of this scheme until a month ago."

Brighton jumped in hard, "I'd put a muzzle on the criticism, Charlie. You let that attitude be known publicly and you'll be cutting your own throat."

Simmons rethought his position. "Sorry." He dropped his casual manner and pulled out his phone. He opened the notebook application and read, "They signed a sales agreement last month for their Scratchpad Interface. Since it requires only a tablet and an app, one that enables certain pre-existing tablet capabilities, it's basically a no-brainer. Over a million app downloads took place the first day it was available. Today there are something like ten million working Scratchpad Interfaces in the U.S. alone, with a hundred-thousand of them in libraries. Dutton's voice unit, what they're calling the *Foxtail*, requires a special chip—they'll be trickling onto the market in the next several weeks. Sizable quantities might be available by the holidays. Dutton's Foxtail may also be used on some tablets, with the proper app."

Brighton asked, "How are you getting such inside information?"

"Most of it is public knowledge. But with national security at stake..."

Brighton cut Simmons off, "National security be damned. If you're smart, Charlie, you'll stop spying on Dutton and his people."

President Forester said, "I agree with your mandate to operate independently, Charlie—but you might want to rethink any active intelligence-gathering on the Duttons, unless you have good reason to believe they're breaking the law."

"Yes, Mr. President."

Forester added, "So what else have you learned?"

"Everything else I have has been available to the press. Dutton has applied for patents in his own name, not his wife's."

"You know, Charlie," said Brighton. "It's interesting to note that Dutton's gotten through to you too."

"Really? How's that?"

"In the same conversation, you describe these events as a scheme and yet repeatedly refer to Dutton as a living person.

Simmons shrugged. "What can I say?"

"Please continue," said Forester.

"Yes, Sir. Um, let's see. You're aware of their original bulletin board for messages to the other side, on the walls of a New Mexico junior college gym." Forester nodded. "Well, with the Scratchpad so broadly available, they've had to expand the gym bulletin board concept to include all junior colleges in the state of New Mexico."

Secretary Cannon exclaimed, "This is *all* so amazing! I'm planning on tapping Ambassador Sherman's expertise on an ongoing basis. Dutton has provided him with everything he needs to continue as before."

The President turned to Senator Brighton and asked, "Bill, do you think I could make it stick if I announced that Sherman will remain our U.N. Ambassador?"

"I'd love to see you do that. What a great precedent that would set. I don't think your opposition would dare counter such a move, not with public opinion being what it is."

"Good," said Forester, "we'll announce it today!"

"And you know what?" said Brighton. "I'm going to bet that, in the end, the dead will be back on the voting rolls."

"You think so?" asked the President.

"I'd bet my life on it. Won't that make for one helluva turn in political history?"

"You're right, Bill," said Cannon. "This opens a whole new spectrum of possibilities, in every conceivable sense."

"Hmmm," said Forester. "Well, was that all you had, Charlie?"

"Not quite, Ted. It now seems likely that the death and kidnapping preceding the interviews were masterminded by Malcolm Claridge."

"Shouldn't I know that name?" asked Forester.

"Possibly," replied Charlie Simmons. "We had evidence he was implicated in an international organ poaching scheme two years ago. When the government's only material witness wound up dead the night before he was to testify before a federal grand jury, the case fell apart. Claridge is the big cheese benefactor of the University's

Med School there in Albuquerque. Big money buys big influence. They don't dare close a door without asking him first."

"Really?"

"Yes," said Simmons. "And there's good reason to believe he's involved in the death of at least four others. The first two were his own henchmen, found bound and shot outside of town.

"The others, the hospital's Psych Department Director and his wife, disappeared while on vacation. Two Indian boys discovered their bodies in the twisted remains of their car, just off the interstate, at the bottom of a canyon in southern Utah."

"Oh, my God," said Ted Forester. "Will Claridge be charged?"

"It's possible, though unlikely," said Simmons. Claridge is in bad shape. He's been laid up for months now, after a broken hip, followed by several strokes. Today, he can't even speak. Anyway, that's all I have for now, Ted."

"Thank you, Charlie," said Forester. "I'd like your people to monitor anyone acting against Dutton. I want his people unharmed."

"I don't think I follow you."

"I'm not certain of your personal views, Charlie, but our discussion has helped me appreciate the importance of these developments. Dutton's technology is likely the most significant innovation in modern times, probably in all of human history. We're at a crossroads, and we have a choice. Do you follow me, Charlie?"

"Yes," said Director Simmons. "Yes, I do, Mr. President."

"My choice is to do what I can. I'm going to ask you to take any resources you need, I'd like you to prevent any and all interference with Dutton or his people, from any quarter. And that includes from within the administration. And you know who I mean."

Simmons knew right away who Forester was referring to. "Yes, Sir."

"Do you feel the high purpose in this, Charlie? Can't you feel it in your belly, like when we flew together in the war?" Forester was rolling. The old fire had returned. "Can you? Will you do this for me, for all of us, Charlie?"

"I can, Mr. President. I will. I'll do whatever it takes."

Chapter 12

It was early September. A little red Alpha was threading its way up a mountain road east of Santa Fe. Marsha Gambles was driving. Miles later, on the far side of the ridge, she finally stopped at a heavy iron gate blocking her advance. The remotely-controlled gate opened and she continued. After the gate, the route became much more precipitous, being cut directly into the mountain face with a sheer drop below. Several miles later, Marsha reached the valley floor. She crossed a bridge over a roaring stream and finally reached a clearing.

Marsha continued toward a razor-wire fence encircling a huge, heavily-reinforced, concrete dome in the final stages of construction. Heavy concrete barriers, rather like a concrete stockade, surrounded the structure. Marsha pulled up to the gate and stopped beside an armored camera enclosure.

From its speaker came Sarah Dutton's voice, "Hi, Marsha. Please follow the drive to the back of the building."

"Hi, Sarah. Thanks."

The powered gate pulled away and Marsha drove into the compound, past a second heavily-armored gate in the shield wall, and around to the building's rear. A man in a hard hat waved her through a huge door into the structure and indicated where she should park. Marsha waved in thanks.

Inside, the building encompassed an area roughly that of a football field. Marsha parked near one of two gaping, armored, silo openings in the floor. She exited her car, dared to step up to the yawning hole, and looked down—down into a gloomy darkness whose bottom seemed hundreds of feet beneath her. She could hear workmen and equipment at their labors far below.

From a smaller such opening nearby, Marsha heard Sarah's voice, "What do you think?"

"Lord, Sarah! Looks like you're ready for a nuclear war. It's an old missile site, isn't it?"

"Yeah." Sarah approached Marsha. "We had to get out of the city." She reached Marsha and they hugged. "Security had become impossible. Too many incidents, even with the police at our home around the clock." Sarah nodded toward the hole beside them. "Pretty scary, huh?"

Marsha stepped back. "Yes! It's making me dizzy. What does Jessica think of all this?"

"She understands. Attending school had become a nightmare, with a police escort and all. So, Judy began home-schooling her in town, and now here. Judy loves being with children; she's a wonderful teacher. She was teaching grade school when she lost *her* little one—before she gave up teaching to do social work. I'm so glad she's back at it with Jessica. She has such a gift. She's even teaching Jessy to speak French."

"That's wonderful," said Marsha. "I'm glad things are working out for you up here." Sarah was smiling as Marsha had never seen her smile. Sarah really was happy, and she so deserved it.

"Things happen for a reason," said Sarah. "Who would have figured? It's so cute to watch Jessica and Judy together in their classroom. Jessica doesn't need a foxtail to converse with Judy, or with her dad, but to me she's just talking with someone I can't see or hear. It's so remarkable watching her sitting alone in an empty room conversing in French. So amazing...our life now. Who'd have guessed Judy would become my very best friend, like the sister I never had."

"I'm glad for you, having a sister makes such a difference. I'm very close to mine too."

Sarah took Marsha by the arm and said, "Let's go on down."

They stepped down the stairway Sarah had scaled moments earlier, and disappeared beneath the surface. Inside, they descended the silo's steel-mesh stairs and soon reached a landing.

Far below were the workmen's lights and the silo floor. Marsha held tight to a handrail along the wall. They entered a cramped little four-man elevator. Sarah closed the door, pressed a button, and they began their descent. Sarah said, "It's so big down here that Jessica and I sometimes wear our roller skates. Or she rides her bike. It's great exercise. Actually, she's trying to talk us into getting some horses."

"I'm with her...*that* would be fun!"

They reached the bottom and exited the little elevator. Half a dozen workmen were busy installing electrical wiring in several areas of the huge silo cavern. Marsha walked out beneath one of the open silo covers high above them, and looked up. "It's not so scary from down here." She looked around, taking in the true dimensions of the space. "Oh my gosh, this place is immense, this is so unreal!"

"We're two hundred feet below the surface."

Sarah led her toward their living area, still some distance away. As they passed the opening of a huge tunnel, Sarah said, "It leads up to the surface, like a giant corkscrew in huge arcs round and round."

They passed through a double doorway protected by heavy, sliding steel doors and entered a corridor. A man in a black jumpsuit, wearing a ball cap with the letters FBI, approached them. He had a pistol holstered across his shoulder. Sarah said, "Hi, Pete."

Pete tipped his hat and smiled. "Good afternoon, ladies."

In a hushed voice Marsha asked, "FBI?"

"Pete is one of the two agents the President sent us."

In the Dutton's living room, a big video screen acted as their living room window. The camera feeding the screen was watching bees and butterflies in the meadow outside the compound fence. It panned left and then right, following the little foragers as they moved between the flowers. Other such screens acted as windows elsewhere within their new quarters.

They seated themselves on a sofa. Marsha said, "It's lovely. This is so much like your home in Albuquerque."

"Thanks, I'm working on it. I'm still hoping life will settle down sometime soon, so we can go back to our home in town. Life here is interesting enough, but I don't think it could possibly be good for Jessica to have to live long-term in what is essentially an air-raid shelter. She hasn't said anything, but I know she's missing her friends and a normal life." Sarah looked at her watch. "Dan should be here any minute."

The screen of the foxtail on a nearby coffee table lit up. "Hi, Marsha." It was Daniel Dutton's voice.

"Hi, Dan. Thanks for having me out."

"How was your drive?"

"Beautiful. Especially down here in your valley."

"So, what's going on?"

"It's President Forester I've come about."

"Forester? How so?"

"Well, you know he has lots of support because of his views regarding your work. It's amazing how quickly the public has accepted all of this." Marsha's voice quivered as she said, "I never would have guessed..." Tears streamed down her cheeks and sobs tugged at her breath.

Sarah reached over and placed her hand on Marsha's, then handed her a tissue.

Marsha continued, "I can't thank you enough for what your work has brought me. I received a message from my father. He's been gone for three years now. I imagine Sarah might understand how it's affected me, not to mention my mom."

"I do," said Sarah. "It's wonderful."

"It is." Marsha sniffled and said, "I've...I've come because I think Forester is in physical danger."

"From Sheets?" asked Dan.

"No, it's Baills."

"Baills?"

"Uh-huh. Vice President Baills, the preacher's son. You remember how he wound up on the ticket at the last minute after Brad Newcomb's death. Well, the old talk is back—that he actually has radical leanings. I think it means something, especially now that the President's support for you is part of the equation."

"You think Baills is moving against the President?"

"It'd be out of character if he didn't. You remember how his old mentor, Josh Fields, died in a kitchen accident—with Baills being appointed to sit out the remainder of his term in the House. And then there's Brad Newcomb, dying of a rare form of botulism—just before he was to be announced as Forester's running mate."

"I see what you mean."

"That's why I feel it's imperative that you get involved."

"Me?"

"Forester's out on a limb. He's extremely vulnerable. Either I'm completely nuts, or our President is in mortal danger. And you're the only person who can really get at the truth."

Marsha and ten-year-old Jessica were sitting on a bench in the corridor between the new quarters and the silo cavern. Her collie was stretched out on the floor beside them. Marsha was putting on a pair of inline roller skates. Jessica already had hers on. Marsha said, "I don't know if I'm up to this, honey. I haven't worn skates in decades."

"You'll be okay. My mom hadn't either, but now she skates all the time. It's great exercise."

They stood up. Marsha was wobbly at first, but didn't fall. She cautiously followed Jessica down a side corridor.

"This is fun!"

"I knew you'd like it," said Jessica.

Terra barked in agreement.

"Terra likes it too."

They paused in the engineering space, a side cavern where the power-generation, environmental, distillation, and auxiliary systems all hummed away. Then they entered a huge cavern, larger in area than the silo bay but much less than half the height.

Jessica said, "This is one of my favorite places. Daddy says they stored Jeeps, trucks, and provisions here—even helicopters—in case of a nuclear war."

"It's enormous!"

"Yeah. They used huge mining machines to dig the caverns out. This is where Terra and I play Frisbee. Jerry taught me how to throw a boomerang down here."

Marsha smiled, "Did he now?"

"Uh-huh. There's quite a trick to it. I've gotten pretty good. It comes right back to me. And I catch it."

"I wonder how they ever got the mining machines in and out?"

"Oh, that's easy," said Jessica. "They used that big winding tunnel out of the silo bay, it goes up to the surface."

"That's right, your mom pointed it out. Near the elevator door."

"Yeah. It opens just above what's left of the old creek—more like a stream now. Daddy said they diverted it to the other side of the valley, back when they built this place, to keep from flooding the underground. When the snow melts in the mountains or there are storms, it's like a rapids over there."

"I saw it. It's beautiful."

"I love it. We still have enough water over here that we have frogs and minnows, and even crayfish in our little stream in the back. Oh, I saw a heron there yesterday! It's really neat. There are humungous sliding doors up there on the platform. That's where I go out, when I take Terra on walks in the woods. Oh, and at night, there's a great view of the sky. It gets so dark, you can almost reach out and touch the Milky Way. I love all the creatures and plants along the stream. I wish my grandpa was here, to walk with me looking for fossils and things, like we did when I was little. Oh, but Judy comes out with me a lot. She's very sweet. We spend a lot of time together. She's my teacher."

"That's what your mom said. And you're learning French."

Jessica smiled and said, "*J'aime le Français!*" And giggled.

The gates opened and Marsha's little red Alpha left the compound and headed up the mountain road out of the valley. After Marsha had passed through the mountain gate and was back on the county road, a large, sinister-looking black van began following her. She glanced into her rear view mirror just as the van rammed her rear bumper. Marsha screamed. She looked again and saw that the occupants of the van were wearing ski masks.

Marsha stepped on the gas, but soon had to slow down for an approaching hairpin turn. When the road straightened out, she accelerated—it seemed like she might get away. A quick look in her rearview mirror proved otherwise, the van was quickly closing.

There was a turnout ahead on her right. Just as she reached it, the van pulled beside her in the oncoming lane.

Marsha stepped on the gas. The van matched her speed and swerved against her little car, forcing her into the turnout. It remained beside her, preventing her escape. There was no way out. The end of the turnout was seconds away. She jumped on the brakes, but was too late. Marsha screamed and covered her eyes as the turnout ended. Her car left the pavement and began a trajectory down the side of the mountain.

Chapter 13

Vice President Morgan Baills wasn't hard to locate; Marsha Gambles had shown Dan a press copy of his itinerary. He caught up with Baills during an appearance at one of the not-so-consequential public functions that were the standard lot of vice presidents.

Baills was twenty years younger than Forester, of rather slight build, with thick blond hair. His strikingly pale-blue eyes gave his gaze an otherworldly quality. Educated at a midwestern evangelical college, and being the son of a nationally-popular fundamentalist minister, he chose politics over the ministry.

Held in high regard by the followers of a conservative fundamentalist movement, with membership in the millions, and being his father's son, Baills seemed a logical choice for Vice President following the untimely death of Brad Newcomb.

On that particular night, Baills was speaking at a veterans' banquet in Minneapolis. Even at a distance, it was obvious the man was not what he otherwise appeared to be. Dan kept his distance, getting no closer than necessary to monitor the man's conversation and thoughts. Baills was extremely intelligent, but most of his intellect was preoccupied with a complex system of schemes within schemes, lies within lies.

To a being such as Dan, unencumbered by the necessity of viewing existence by corporeal means, Baills was a man walking about with dense black clouds around him. The phenomenon wasn't unique in Dan's experience, many had some degree of palpable spiritual baggage they toted about.

But only with Malcolm Claridge, a murderous old wreck of a man, had Dan seen anything reminiscent of what was before him. As repulsive as he was, Claridge had nothing like the tangle of spiritual filth Dan sensed around Baills. At close quarters, the spiritual stench of the man was so repulsive as to be all but overpowering.

Those around Baills had no appreciation of who or what they were really dealing with. Things happened about him inexplicably, in which the good works of honest men were twisted and warped into something else, while the lies and manipulations of Baills' vile class brought them wealth and power.

Baills' conversation was innocuous enough, yet Dan caught glimpses of destruction past and future in the mind of a man with aspirations to someday rule the world at any cost.

Even so, Baills was a coward. Nothing he did was in the open—he acted solely through others. All the while, he was cool and very much in control, and at little risk of giving himself away. And the schemes turned and turned. Baills found it amusing how gullible and trusting the cattle about him were.

It was later that night in Minneapolis, aboard *Air Force Two*, that Dan caught what he'd been waiting for. Over a scrambled vidphone line, alone in his cabin, Baills made a call to a man Dan didn't recognize.

"Red Man?"

"Hello, sir." The person in the video image was a bespectacled little weasel of a man in a three-piece suit, wearing a less-than-convincing hairpiece. He nervously tugged at his right ear lobe. An American flag stood proudly behind him in the corner of the room.

Baills said, "I'm shutting off my video pick-up."

"Good idea, sir."

Baills poked a finger at a control on his vidphone console and the pick-up's red pilot light went dark. "I hope there's no chance of our conversation being picked up on your end."

"No chance at all, sir. It's a scrambled signal and this room is completely shielded. I've got a hush field around my desk. Besides, my vidphone's speaker has a strictly conical focus and I'm just inside it. Yours should be the same. No one else can possibly hear anything you're saying. Someone sitting in front of my desk couldn't even hear me.

"Okay, what have you got for me?"

"Well, sir, we really must act soon. I've been waiting for your call, but it never came. We've had the man we need for weeks now, and he has access. As we agreed, I won't burden you with his name or position, or the location. But no one stays bought forever. We either need to go ahead or give it up, sir."

"Is he clean enough for our purposes?"

"Spotless, sir," said Red Man. "Hector found him. He's a career man with appetites he can't afford."

"Does he know what's expected of him?" asked Baills.

"Yes, sir. He's very familiar with the subject and its safeguards. He understands that, once it's in place and switched on, the device will activate itself at the appropriate time. And he has the means to insure he'll be out of the area."

"Has he been paid?"

"He has a deposit receipt for a million sitting in a Venezuelan bank," replied Red Man. "Plus the $100,000 in gold he's holding."

"Who else knows of this?"

"Just like we'd planned, sir. Only Hector and Ringer."

"And Sheets," said Baills.

"You mean Elmer, don't you, sir?" Red Man tugged at his ear again.

Baills looked pained. "Uh, sorry. Elmer."

"Of course Elmer knows, it's his money."

"I hope you've kept him out of this as much as possible," admonished Baills.

"He knows nothing of the particulars, sir. I'm his sole contact and that's only been twice, on a secure voice line."

"Then who all knows I'm involved?"

"Just me, Hector, and Elmer. Ringer knows only Hector, and Hector is our new recruit's only contact."

Baills said, "I hope you and Hector have all the kinks worked out of this. We won't get a second chance. There's too much riding on this for a screw-up."

"I can't give you any guarantees, sir," said Red Man. Our chances get worse every day. But the Bureau won't be a problem. Director Simmons is too busy trying to keep up with the demonstrations Elmer's people are making all over the place. Three hundred of them have been jailed. They're hitting the White House very heavily now, as I'm certain you're aware, but I'm afraid some of those screwball followers of his will try something on their own.

"My boys won't be a problem—they haven't got a clue. Just babes in the woods. This new guy has been under their noses for years. Once we get started, the Old Man will have very little chance of escaping what's coming. As you suggested and I agree, the less you know now, the better off you'll be afterward. With your approval, sir, we'll proceed at the first opportunity. Everything is in place. When it's done, the rest will be up to you and Hector."

"Very well," said Baills, "go ahead. As you say, we'd better do it now or give it up. There's too much to lose if we give it up. I just hadn't expected popular support to be so intense. And I think it's best that you and I not speak again until I get you into the Bureau Directorship."

Red Man smiled and tugged at his ear. "Agreed, sir."

Baills hit the vidphone controls and broke the connection. The screen faded to black.

Chapter 14

It was after midnight and Dan needed to act quickly. He had to locate someone who would listen to him, someone who had access to the President.

Sarah was still up. She woke Jerry, in his apartment down the corridor from their new underground digs, and Dan explained the situation. Sarah got on the phone to contact Marsha Gambles. Dan set Jerry to contacting Senator Brighton.

Pete popped in and said, "I'm sorry to disturb you this late, but I thought you should know. Ben and I have just been recalled. Personally, I feel it's an illegal order, especially since we were posted here at the President's request. Something's wrong, I don't feel Director Simmons would have sanctioned such an order. Anyway, I'm staying put. Ben has returned to the Santa Fe office. I'm available if you need anything. I'll be on patrol when I'm not in my quarters."

"Thanks, Pete," said Dan. "We really do appreciate it."

Pete hefted his assault weapon to indicate his heightened sense of readiness. He then warned, "I think it'd be a good idea if you armed yourselves, especially if you'll be leaving the silo. I have extra weapons, just in case you aren't sufficiently equipped." As Pete turned to leave, he raised his walkie-talkie and added, "If you can't reach me on this, I have my foxtail." He smiled and patted the interface in his breast pocket, then departed, closing the door.

Dan remarked, "Pete's a good man. I should have expected this. At least now we know the FBI's involved and not to be trusted."

In Bethesda, Helen Brighton approached her sleeping husband. She placed her hand on his shoulder and whispered, "Bill, honey, wake up. You have a phone call."

"Huh? Who...who's calling at this hour?"

"It's Daniel Dutton."

A bleary-eyed Senator Brighton sat down at his desk and tried to focus on the vidphone image. In the image, there was a commotion going on in the Dutton living room.

Sarah was at the kitchen doorway, waving for Jerry to come her way, "Jerry, can you come in here a moment?"

Jerry said, "Just a moment, Senator, here's Dan." He hit the vidphone controls and said, "Sure, Sarah." Then disappeared into the kitchen.

Dan picked up the vidphone line, "Hello, Senator. Sorry we got you up at this hour. I have something extremely important to share with you."

"That's what Jerry Sterling said. By all means, please tell me."

"I've just uncovered a conspiracy to assassinate President Forester."

That woke Brighton. He rubbed his weary eyes and shook his head in disappointment. "I suspected this was coming. How'd you find out?"

"It wasn't hard, Senator, considering."

"I can imagine. I've warned Forester that this was a possibility. Excuse me a moment." To someone off screen he asked, "Could you please get me a cup of black coffee? No...make it a pot. I can see I'm going to need to stay awake." He turned back to the vidphone pick-up. "Now don't tell me. Morgan Baills."

"That's right. Baills and someone who spoke like he was an official within the security community. They used code names; they're planning to set some sort of device."

"A bomb?"

Dan shared what he'd overheard, and about Pete's ordered recall.

Sarah stepped into the vidphone camera's field of view. "Excuse me, Senator. I'm Dan's wife, Sarah. I felt this was important for you to know. We just learned that Marsha Gambles was injured in an auto accident. She was returning to Santa Fe, after her visit here with us this afternoon."

"How is she?" asked Brighton.

"I just spoke with her producer, Peg, at the hospital in Santa Fe. Marsha's in fair condition, with a concussion and multiple contusions. She's been unconscious, but finally came around about four hours after her rescue. Otherwise, Peg says Marsha's okay. She'll be in the hospital another four or five days. Her little sports car had been forced off the mountain road and over the edge. Miraculously, it was caught in midair by a large tree before it could fall down the side of the mountain. Some locals spotted it an hour or so later; as you can imagine, her rescue was anything but routine."

"What an amazing story." said Brighton. "I'm happy she'll be okay."

"Me too," said Sarah. "Jerry's leaving for the hospital now. Our cellular service has been off most of the evening, and Dan has been away, or we might have known earlier. Our daughter, Jessica, has been saying all evening that something was wrong with Marsha—so now we know. Anyway, that's it. Thanks, Senator." Sarah waved and retreated from view.

"Thank you, Sarah. From what you've both said, Daniel, this has all the earmarks of a well-orchestrated conspiracy. I'm not surprised your phones have become an issue, with the agents being recalled, and Marsha Gambles' accident. I think these are signs of things to come."

"I'm afraid you're right, Senator," said Dan. "I'll stay as close to home as I can. Though these might also be attempts to distract us from events away from home. I'll have to keep better tabs on our extended family. There's an awful lot going on just now."

"I hope you're well-provisioned, Daniel, and can operate somewhat independently in that rabbit warren of yours. If they're successful in an assassination attempt, you might expect an outright attack."

"I can feel it coming," said Dan. "I'm going to see what can be done to get some help up here. You'd be surprised how many supporters we have among the public."

"No, I wouldn't. You today are perhaps our civilization's most admired and valued individual. Your supporters must honestly number in the billions. I can't think of anything more important to your contemporaries than supporting your goals."

"Thank you, Senator, I'm only doing what I feel is right. Your support means a great deal to us."

The senator smiled and said, "So...who else have you called?"

"You're the first. I figured that out of your mouth, the story would have a certain credibility—especially since it concerns Baills. If word gets to him, there's no telling what might happen."

"Good thinking, you're right," agreed Brighton. "They'd have to take a senior senator seriously, whatever the subject might be."

"Then you'll be calling the Secret Service and Forester?"

"Absolutely. If the Bureau has pulled their men, something's going on right under Charlie Simmons' nose. He and Forester are old friends. Forester gave him direct orders to do whatever was necessary to protect your interests. Charlie needs to be told, but cautioned to proceed carefully. I'll call him last, since it's the Secret Service that's directly charged with protecting the safety of the President."

Dan added, "You need to tell them the person they're looking for is someone who has regular access to Forester and his environment."

"I will. We'll have to hope that some of the people protecting Forester are still loyal. By the level of the conspirators' attempts at secrecy, I'd bet there are damned few involved. Or they wouldn't be so paranoid about being detected."

"Do we know where to find the President?"

"He's in L.A. I've been trying to keep in touch with him, or at least know his itinerary, with all the uproar we're having in D.C."

"I could actively help," said Dan, "if we can get an interface out to him."

"That's a great idea. Ted's staying at a hotel with his full Secret Service contingent."

"Why don't I go ahead and locate him, while you start making your calls? See if someone can get a foxtail out to him ASAP. With Jerry on his way to the hospital in Santa Fe, he could give them his device. I do think it might be wise to remove Forester from his normal environment until we can get a handle on things."

"You're right," agreed Brighton. "What a great idea. I'll recommend that, and we'll get a device out to Ted immediately—and get your technology working for us. I'll start making my calls and get back to you in a bit."

"Thank you, Senator."

"Good bye, Daniel. I'll keep you posted." Brighton disconnected.

Dan found Ted Forester in no time, and quickly scoped out what the President was up to that day. Forester had his wife with him and had scheduled speeches at several major conventions in the city. They also had plans to visit an old political ally in the hospital.

Forester found it tiresome making two coast-to-coast trips in the same day, so their routine amounted to sleeping over when at all possible. The President had never been much of a fan of air travel, even though he'd been a combat pilot for six years. He maintained that it wasn't flying that bothered him, but the fact that the only time he'd been shot down in four hundred missions had been when someone else was at the controls.

The vidphone rang and a man on the other end said, "Secret Service, Shift Leader Folkes here."

"Agent Folkes, this is Senator Brighton. I need to speak with the President and Wally Harris, your Special Agent in Charge. This is of grave importance. It can't wait. I don't have time to explain this to anyone else."

Agent Folkes said, "I have the Deputy I.C. right here, sir."

"That won't do! I'm only going to say this one more time. Get me the President and Harris. Now!"

"Yes, sir." Folkes pushed his mute button and spoke to someone in the room. He released it and said, "They'll be with you in just a few moments, Senator."

"Thank you."

Forester and Special Agent Harris were staring at a vidphone screen in a room adjoining the Presidential Suite. Brighton and Forester were each still in their robes. "...I guess that's about all we know, Ted," said Brighton. "I'd suggest using discretion in passing any of this along. With Charlie's men being ordered out of Dutton's new place, it's hard to know who's involved. In my mind, the Secret Service should give themselves some pretty serious scrutiny too. If the person out to do this has been around you for years, undetected, you have to question how effective the Service has been in their mission."

"You're obviously right, Bill," said Ted Forester, "but let me talk with Charlie Simmons. I'm certain that anything going on is totally beyond his knowledge."

"That's my thinking too."

Wally Harris said, "I do need to report this to my superior, Mr. President. And our first priority must be to do as Daniel Dutton has suggested, and remove you from your normal environment. Perhaps if you were flown somewhere no one expected and that area was secured, we could eliminate the greatest chance of an attempt being successful. Then, perhaps a group could be formed from outside the Bureau and the Service, to investigate these allegations objectively."

"I agree, Wally," said Forester. "That's a great idea. Go ahead and get Kermit Weller involved and we'll finalize our plans to relocate. But not to D.C. And you can get an investigation started and security redoubled. First though, I want that interface Dan Dutton suggested. Like Senator Brighton said, let's get this technology working for us."

Harris replied, "With the help of the Air Force, I think I can have the device out here by dawn, Sir."

"Excellent!"

Wally Harris rang up his senior in D.C.

Kermit Weller's features glared out of the vidphone screen. "This better be good, Wally, it's 4:00 A.M."

"It's extremely important, sir." Wally described the plot against the President in detail.

When Harris had finished, Weller sat silent for a long moment. He tugged at his ear in a fashion familiar to his colleagues. "It's hard to believe, considering Dutton is the source, but we're forced to take any threat seriously. With the obvious involvement of the FBI, we'll have to take it seriously. And you say the President is going to speak with Director Simmons?"

"That's right, sir."

"Tell you what, Wally—since it's likely that others in the security community are involved, we have to be extremely careful with whom we share this information."

Harris nodded. "I agree, sir. It makes it extremely difficult to know how to proceed."

"Exactly. So leave it up to me. Does anyone outside the Presidential detail in L.A. know about this?"

"No, sir. In fact only the night shift leader, Deputy I.C., and I know anything at all."

"Good," said Weller. "See that it stays that way. Leave the rest to me. At this point we don't know who we can trust. Just do as the President has asked, and keep me informed. I'll get the ball rolling investigating the situation and beefing up security." Weller tugged at his ear. "Where are you taking the President?"

"To an air base somewhere north of Edmonton, Alberta."

"Canada?"

"Yes, sir. It was President Forester's idea. He's already gotten approval from the Canadian Prime Minister. There's to be no public notification of his whereabouts. The press is being told he's staying in L.A. for a few more days. Several of our men are to stay here, to make it look as if the President is still in residence at the hotel."

"Excellent idea—the Old Man is in top form. Even if other agencies found out, they'd have no access to him on a Canadian air base. In D.C., there'd be no stopping them." Weller looked off-screen for a moment. "When is he leaving?"

"Noon today, after breakfast at the hospital with former Governor Jamison."

"Good work, Wally. Who are you leaving behind?"

"My deputy and four agents."

"Good," said Weller. "But I think it'd be best if you had those who know about the conspiracy with you. They may prove valuable. Why not leave one of your assistants instead of your deputy?"

"I see what you mean, sir. I'll do that."

"Keep me informed," said Weller, "and don't assume anyone can be trusted. You might advise the President to do the same. I'll do the rest."

Chapter 15

It was 6:30 in the morning. Air Force Major Brad Weston entered the empty flight deck of the aircraft. Flight orders had just been issued; he only had a few minutes. The flight crew wouldn't start boarding *Air Force One* for some hours yet, but the maintenance crew could show up any minute.

Weston looked out a port-side window toward the nearby maintenance hangar, making certain no one was approaching the aircraft. He was finding it hard to keep the cool head he'd imagined having. His pulse pounded in his ears as he wiped at the sweat dripping from his brow. Weston took several long slow breaths and finally knelt down beside the engineer's console.

A quarter-turn each released the four toggles securing the access cover to the first of the plane's three flight computers. He pulled the panel free and nervously set it aside.

Each of the aircraft's three computers, in daily rotation, controlled the entirety of the flight control systems on its own—while its twins were held in emergency reserve. For added safety, the systems were housed in enclosures positioned well apart from each other in the aircraft.

Weston lifted a pant cuff of his flight suit and removed a device taped to his leg. When he'd finished installing the device he flicked its power switch and replaced the access cover.

A dull metallic clang echoed through the plane just as he tightened the last of the toggles. A cautious look out the window revealed the source, two maintenance crewmen inspecting the innards of the outboard port engine. Weston sighed and shook his head, then ducked down and glanced at his watch. Time was wasting, he still had two computers to go.

Fifteen long minutes later, in the maintenance hangar, Weston swallowed two capsules and washed them down with a can of soda. In a short while, he'd be on his way to the nearest emergency room, too sick to be along for the plane's departure.

Still in his robe after his fourth cup of coffee, Ted Forester got the thrill of his life when he activated the interface. It had been rushed to him in a relay by two helicopters and an Air Force jet. "Are you here, Mr. Dutton?" Forester's smile was incandescent.

"Yes, Mr. President, I'm here. Daniel Dutton at your service." Daniel took a seat near the President and his wife.

"Wow! It's remarkable being able to do this. I've seen your interview with Marsha Gambles several times. And I do recognize your voice, Daniel. We've downloaded several of your audio books. Linda and I both love your work." Forester took a deep breath, paused, and gathered his thoughts. His smile melted away. "But I guess we'd better get to the situation at hand."

"Thank you for the compliment, Mr. President. My wife and I are long-time fans of your work as well. But, yes, let's get down to business."

"Okay. What do you make of this conspiracy, Daniel?"

"It's a real threat, Sir. My hope is that I can help you survive it. The worst part is having no idea regarding where or when. I'm trying to pick up what I can from the people in your party here at the hotel. I haven't detected anything that would indicate any of them are part of some action to harm you. Though, I must admit, I don't know that I really qualify as an extra-corporeal sleuth, but I'm learning. Most people's thoughts and mental pictures are easy to read—though some few are in such a mental state, that it's more like sticking your mind in a blender just trying to fathom their thoughts. I find I'd rather just keep my distance from the worst of them—the devious, evil-minded ones."

"Who, for instance?"

"Morgan Baills."

"I think I know what you mean. There's something about Baills that I've never quite been able to put a finger on. Something that makes me uneasy turning my back to him. He was never my idea of a running mate. I'm convinced now that our taking him on was an ill-conceived expedient to winning the election. And I can't say with any certainty that his presence on the ticket really made any difference. He wasn't my first choice; I often wish we'd done otherwise. The truth is, I like having him around about as much as I'd enjoy wearing a sardine necklace."

Wally Harris smiled and put a finger up to the earpiece in his left ear. "Mr. President, Sir. I'm sorry to cut you off, but it's time for us to start getting ready. We'll have to make our way to the chopper soon. After your breakfast with the Governor, we'll have to rush to El Toro for our flight north."

"Very well, Wally." Forester looked at the interface. "How do we go about this, Daniel?"

"I'd suggest you just stick it in your jacket pocket and plug in the earpiece, like Wally is doing with his radio."

Moments later, Forester was on the phone with Director Simmons. Simmons was saying, "If it's true, Ted, where do we start? They're my people."

"All you can do, Charlie, is decide whom you trust and act accordingly."

"Of course," agreed Simmons, "you're right. I'll do everything I can, but I'd also advise Wally Harris to keep Bureau people away from you. Don't take any chances, Ted. With anyone! And keep Wally at your side. He's a good man. *The best*. He'll go down, before he'll let anything happen to you."

Wally Harris stepped up to Forester and said, "Mr. President, Sir. I'm sorry to interrupt you, but the chopper's here."

Later, during the helicopter flight to El Toro Air Station, Ted Forester had a chance to visit with Dan by writing his end of the conversation on a paper tablet. The chopper crew knew nothing of the conspiracy or the changes in their itinerary.

Ten minutes out of El Toro, Wally Harris tapped Forester on the shoulder. Ted looked up from his tablet. "I'm sorry to bother you, Sir. But we've just been informed that our plane's flight engineer has fallen ill and won't be able to make the flight. He collapsed while doing his preflight check."

"What's wrong?"

"They think it's appendicitis. Won't know for sure until he makes it to the hospital. It's going to delay our flight, Sir. We'll have to find a suitable replacement."

"I hope Brad's going to be okay. Make sure his wife is informed. I know when my appendix burst, it felt like the end of the world."

"I'll see to it, Sir." Harris got close to Forester and in hushed tones whispered, "I'm going to order a thorough search of the plane for anything suspicious—just in case

Major Weston's illness is in any way connected with the conspiracy." The chopper's noise-cancellation system eliminated the ear-walloping rotor-racket they'd otherwise have endured in a helicopter cabin.

Forester whispered back, "Do you really think that's necessary, Wally? I can't believe Brad Weston would be involved in any such plot."

"I'd be grossly in neglect of my duty to protect you, Mr. President, if I failed to do everything possible to insure your safety."

"How long will it take?"

"Likely two hours, Sir—off the tarmac, in a hangar"

"Two hours! We don't have that kind of time, Wally. And I'd bet El Toro doesn't have anyone experienced with our special systems anyway."

"Likely not, Sir. We'd probably have to fly someone in."

"Wouldn't it do to give the plane the once-over with explosives-sniffing dogs? You could send a chopper out after them."

"Possibly, Sir"

"Then let's do that. Call someone. Maybe at LAX. And let's get on with it."

"All right, Sir," said Wally, reluctantly.

By two that afternoon, Ted Forester had had enough of sitting in the chopper waiting for the inspection to be completed. At 1:30 they'd been informed that Brad Weston had died. A definitive cause wouldn't be known until an autopsy had been performed and tests run, though appendicitis had been ruled out.

At 2:15 they were given the go-ahead. The dog hadn't found any explosives. The chopper started its engines for the short hop from their position out in the middle of the tarmac over to *Air Force One*. When they arrived, Forester took a few minutes on the tarmac and said a long thank you to the German Shepherd before boarding the plane.

The President and his wife took seats in the forward cabin with the rest of the crew and passengers, as far aft as possible, so he could have a little privacy to converse with Daniel Dutton.

They had borrowed a flight engineer from El Toro and everything seemed to be in order.

The pilot gave orders that all on board were to fasten their seat belts—the air would be choppy until they reached their cruising altitude. The plane had been given priority in the scheme of outgoing traffic by the L.A. Control Center.

They taxied into position for takeoff. The pilot revved the engines and the huge plane began its race down the runway.

An instant before the wheels left the ground, Wally Harris rushed into the cabin from the comm center and quickly took a seat across the aisle from the President; his expression was grave. Wally got close to make himself heard above the roar of the jet engines.

"Sir." President Forester looked up. "Mr. President, we just got a priority message from Washington. Director Simmons is dead, Sir. He was in an automobile accident fifteen minutes ago. His car was purposely run off the road."

Forester fought to hold back tears, but they came anyway—he took a deep breath and wiped them from his cheek. *"Dead?"*

"Yes, Sir. He died on the way to the hospital. His driver was killed instantly."

Forester sat silently. After clearing the runway and gaining some altitude, the plane turned westward, toward the ocean, where it could gain sufficient altitude to enter the jetway northward. Forester was staring absently out the nearby window. Soberly, he looked up at Harris and said, "It's started, hasn't it, Wally?"

"I believe it has, Sir."

Now over the ocean, the plane began banking northward.

On the flight deck, the pilot, Air Force Colonel Ike Avery, was at his controls. An alarm began sounding; a red light on his control panel began flashing. "Jesus Christ," said Avery, "we just lost our lead computer!"

Abruptly, the plane began a steep climb. Avery and his copilot, Major Preston, strained forward on their control yokes to force the plane's nose down, but to no avail.

Avery said, "Number two should take control any second now."

Another light on the console began flashing. "It's no use, Ike," said Preston, "Two's gone too!"

A second alarm sounded. Lights began flashing all over the cabin. Avery got up and shifted his attention to a bank of switches, as Preston continued straining at the yoke. Their replacement flight engineer, Marine Major Ace Gorman, approached from his console. His expression was solemn. Avery was futilely flipping switches.

Yelling over the alarms, Gorman exclaimed, "All three of the flight computers are dead!"

Avery replied, "Great! Our elevator controls are completely unresponsive. We're climbing and there's nothing we can do to stop it. Inform the President. I'm calling L.A. Center." Avery took his seat, reached toward his control radio console, and pressed a button. Through the mic on his headset, he said, "L.A. Center, this is *Air Force One*. We're in serious trouble. Repeat, we're in serious trouble. Over."

Back in the passenger cabin, the alarm was sounding. Gorman rushed down the stairs from the flight deck and picked up the public address microphone. The alarm fell silent. "This is Major Gorman, your flight engineer. We've had a serious computer systems failure. We're trying to manage control without it. But servo-systems normally controlled by the computers aren't responding to manual control. Please stay in your seats!" He returned the mike to its place on the bulkhead and looked at the President. The alarm resumed sounding. He stepped up close to Forester and said, as softly as he could, "I'm sorry, Sir, but the controls for your escape pod have been rendered useless as well."

"Thank you, Major."

The major turned away and rushed back up the stairs. Pandemonium overtook the forward cabin.

Wally Harris turned to his President and said, "I'm sorry, Sir."

"Don't blame yourself, Wally. You've done all you could and more. Thank you." Forester saw tears in Harris' eyes. He knew the man had done his best and that he was crushed by the realization that he'd failed his President.

Linda Forester began crying. It seemed that everyone, except for the Secret Service and some of the military personnel, had lost control. Several people were running about, frantic to find a way to free themselves from the inevitable.

Avery's voice replaced the alarm. "Prepare yourselves for the worst. All our control systems have failed. Soon we'll enter a stall from which we have little hope of recovering. Air traffic personnel have notified the Coast Guard. Please take your seats. Grab the flotation device from beneath your seat and put it on. Then secure your seatbelts, lean forward, place your head on your knees, and cover your head with your arms." The alarm resumed.

On the flight deck, another alarm began sounding that could easily be heard down the stairs. The copilot turned to Avery and said, "That's the stall warning, Ike. We're screwed!"

Ted Forester knew a stall warning from his days as a combat pilot. The wings were losing their bite on the air; soon the plane would lose all lift and would tumble out of control.

Above the screams and alarms, Forester heard the calm voice of his new friend coming from the earpiece still hanging over his right ear. He pressed the earpiece against his ear and tried to ignore the pandemonium around him. "Ted, try to keep your cool. Put on your life jackets."

It took what seemed forever for Ted to help his wife into her life jacket. By the time he'd started putting on his own, the plane's angle above the horizontal had become so critical that finally its wings provided no lift at all. The huge plane began falling.

The alarms ceased—abruptly the people around Ted fell silent. The pilot's voice sounded again, "Assume your crash positions. We have about three minutes before we'll be in the water. Get out of the plane as soon as you can, and get away. The Coast Guard will be along soon to pick us up." The tumult returned. Many again left their seats.

Ted knew it was unlikely any of them would survive, but it was the kindest thing the pilot could have said. People needed hope. Daniel Dutton's voice returned to the earpiece. "Unplug your earpiece from the phone, so the others can hear me."

Forester answered, "Okay, Daniel," and did so.

Wally Harris had been watching. He raised his voice and said, "Hey! All of you! Quiet down and listen to this. It's important."

Daniel's voice came from the foxtail phone's speaker. "Take a few deep breaths, Ted. All of you."

A woman in a panic a few seats away said, "That, that voice...who is that?"

Wally answered so all could hear, "It's *Daniel Dutton*. Listen!"

Daniel continued, "Allow yourselves to back off a little. Don't be afraid. I'll be here with you." The plane continued its slow spin as they fell toward the sea.

Forester took several deep breaths, then turned to his wife. She was silent. He gave her a warm kiss on the cheek. "I love you, Linda. Did you hear Daniel? Let's take several deep breaths. Let's not be afraid. He'll be with us. We'll be okay. At least now we have some hope." He took her hand.

"I love you, Ted." Her face was wet with tears, but a sober resolve had replaced her grief.

"Ted," continued Daniel, "All of you. We've only got a minute. Listen to me! There's nothing to fear. Honestly, it's almost like diving into a pool. Now, when I tell you—take a deep breath and hold it. It'll be over in a moment."

There was a short silence.

"Ted. Everyone."

"Yes, Daniel."

"Take that deep breath and hold it. Stay with me."

They all took a deep breath. And just as they began to hold it, it happened.

In a blink it was over.

They felt little. There was no time to feel.

There was water everywhere. And wreckage. The plane had been torn open in front of them, and again behind the wings. Air and jet fuel bubbled from the broken pieces of the twisted hulk. Somehow, fire had started about the large central section, even as it sank.

Not a single voice could be heard.

Ted watched it all. He was floating above it, just as if he were dangling beneath some giant balloon. He looked up. There was no balloon.

Bodies and pieces of bodies bobbed about among bits and pieces of the great plane. Ted felt an overwhelming sadness at the loss, an almost beautiful sadness. He lifted his gaze from the wreckage and found a warm something reaching out to him. A familiar something. A something he should recognize. It was his friend, Daniel. And somehow he heard a voice that said, "Hello, my friend." When he saw Daniel's kind face smiling at him, he knew everything would be all right.

"Daniel...it's you, Daniel!" Somehow he'd said it, but he hadn't.

"It's me, Ted, and Linda is here with us. It wasn't all that bad, was it? You survived."

Yes, Ted *had* survived. "You're right." And he could sense Linda's presence too. "Shouldn't we do something, Daniel? Shouldn't we wait for the boats?"

"There's no need, Ted. There's no need. Reach out to me and hold my hand."

"Hold your hand? I thought..." He reached out and felt Daniel reaching to him. "I can. I can feel your hand."

"Good, now hang on. I don't want to lose you."

Ted hung on. In a blink they were somewhere else.

Chapter 16

It was six o'clock the morning of the day after. An unshaven Senator Brighton pulled a prepaid throwaway cellphone from his pants pocket and commenced dialing. He was wearing a ball cap, a threadbare flannel shirt, and old jeans. Helen Brighton was in curlers and a gray sweatsuit. She held the handle of a two-wheeled cart as she sat beside her husband on a bench in a D.C. Metro subway terminal.

In the living room of the Dutton's underground residence, Daniel answered the phone, "Hi, Senator."

In D.C. the senator said, "Hi, Dan. Now it's me calling you for help."

"What's going on?"

"I guess you could call us fugitives."

"Fugitives?"

"Yep. Our housekeeper informed me that our home was forcibly entered by a group of men that could have been the FBI, though they offered no such identification. Their van was unmarked. This was probably about the same time Baills was sworn in last night."

"Where were you when this happened?"

"Fortunately, I'd taken Helen to a second-rate motel when *Air Force One* was reported down. We spent the night there. Just now we're incognito."

"Tell you what, Senator—don't say a word about your location. Give me a second and I'll find you."

A heartbeat later Daniel said, "Okay. Found you. Just stay there. I'm going to have a friend pick you up. Her name is Roxy."

"We won't move an inch."

"Oh, one more thing. Ted and Linda are here."

A half hour later—wearing tattered jeans, a western shirt tied at her waist, cowboy boots, and an engaging smile—tall, blonde, pony-tailed Roxy Pickett entered the terminal. She walked right past the Brightons, twice, before the Senator reached out and gently grabbed her by the arm.

"Are you looking for us, honey?"

Roxy laughed and under her breath, said, "I hope you're who I think you are." She hugged Brighton and exclaimed out loud, "Uncle Bill!"

"Roxy!"

"How was your trip? It's so good to see you."

At the curb outside the terminal, Roxy slid open the side door of her powder-blue panel van. "I brought some help."

Inside the van, seated on the second of the two bench seats, were two young men —one blonde and muscular with a military haircut, the second Native American and not as big, but wiry.

"So I see," said Brighton. "Hello, gentlemen! Thank you for coming."

"Yes," said Helen Brighton, "Thank you so much."

Brighton hoisted the cart containing their clothes into the van. The young man with the military look hefted it to the extended back end of the vehicle. When he returned he offered his hand and said, "You're very welcome, sir. I'm Steve, Roxy's brother."

The second young man offered his hand as well and said, "I'm honored, sir. Ma'am. I'm Roxy's boyfriend, Sam Redhawk."

"My pleasure, gentlemen."

Roxy reached into the van for her well-worn leather jacket and put it on, then climbed into the driver's seat. The Brightons piled in onto the front bench and buckled up. Sam slid the side door shut.

"Well," said Roxy, buckling her seatbelt. "Where would you like to go, Senator?"

"Well...to be honest...New Mexico."

"Wah-hoo!" yelled Steve.

Smiling, Roxy said, "We hoped you'd say that. You'll have to excuse Steve, Senator. He just mustered out of the Marine Corps last week, and he's hoping for a fight up there in the mountains."

"Well," said Brighton, "I certainly hope you'll be disappointed, young man."

"Either way," said Roxy, "we've come prepared." She pointed a thumb toward the back end of the vehicle, which was chockablock with gear and provisions.

"I'm glad for that," said Brighton.

Roxy went on, "Okay, what would you say if we just pushed on through, driving in shifts, and maybe stopped just once for sleep? That way we'll make it to the valley by tomorrow night."

"Oh, my Lord," said Brighton, "you're serious!"

At about eleven that night they made it to St. Louis, where they laid up for some much-needed sleep. They'd had a long, wearing day. All resolved that the following day they'd get an early start and drive straight through.

Roxy decided it would be wiser to approach the Duttons' from the east, through Terrero rather than Santa Fe, the obvious route along the interstate. On the way, they'd stop and stretch in Liberal, Kansas and plan their approach. Roxy had brought along geological survey maps of the area, in the tightest scale possible. She'd researched the available satellite images of the valley, but the most recent of them had been four years old.

The Brightons learned that their young benefactors had been volunteers to Dutton's cause from the first weeks. Roxy was a registered nurse, an animal rights activist, and a published author. Brighton was much impressed by the level of her accomplishments in a brief twenty-six years.

Steve, twenty-two, was—given the circumstances—understandably full of vinegar and aching for a fight. His Commander-in-Chief, after all, had just been assassinated. Besides the necessary provisions, he'd brought along sufficient arms and ammunition to take on a considerable force.

Sam, the eldest of the three, was a civil engineer and had worked with Roxy and Steve's father, Stacy, until Stacy's death eight months earlier. They'd all lived together on the Pickett's farm near Centreville, Virginia. Roxy had been receiving messages from her deceased father ever since, via a scratchpad interface.

Behind the impressive, vine-covered stone edifice of The Palkin Institute, a television broadcast was being screened in the board room. A male newscaster's voice narrated footage of the retrieval of *Air Force One's* wreckage. "And this is all that remains of *Air Force One* following its crash into the Pacific Ocean yesterday afternoon. Divers located the black box and flight recorder this morning…"

Leonard Palkin clicked the TV's remote and the audio fell silent. He addressed the four men seated before him at the huge table. "Yesterday's events represent only the first return on our investment, gentlemen. Sheets has proven an eminently wise choice as our conduit. And he's done well at distracting attention from Baills', and our activities."

Jonas Weemer, the bearded man to Palkin's left, said, "The question is, Leonard, can the idiot keep up the racket long enough for Baills to dig Dutton's bunch out of their hole? They have to be dealt with before Baills' position is totally compromised. As for Sheets, mark my words—in the end, the man will be nothing but a liability."

Across the table, Dimitri Lozoff, a bald man with a thin little mustache, pounded the table with his fist. "All good points, Jonas, but there are still the pesky college bulletin boards, and the paltry issue that Dutton's infernal scratchpad technology is already in the hands of millions by now. Our position is rapidly becoming totally untenable. You've seen how this technology has eroded the public's confidence in us. This entire situation was allowed to get too far out of hand before action was taken against Forester."

Palkin shook his head. "There's actually little to get worked up about, Dimitri. Baills has just signed an emergency Presidential order prohibiting the sale, distribution, or possession of the devices. All U.S. warehousing and manufacturing facilities for the voice device are being seized at this very moment. And the old network is applying pressure on the E.U. Council, for actions at the plant and warehouse in Cologne."

Mortimer Banic, seated next to Lozoff, said, "I wish them luck with that, Leonard. Next to the French, the Germans are the least likely to surrender to outside pressure of any sort."

The heavy-set man at the far end of the huge table began laughing. It was a sinister, knowing laugh. When all eyes were finally on him, he stopped. "The lot of you are so thick-headed, you don't understand what you're dealing with."

"I don't believe I follow you, Doctor Banning," said Palkin. "I thought you approved of our actions."

"Theoretically I have, but Dimitri is right. It's too late. Operating through Sheets has left us without any means of reigning in Baills. The man is a damned fool. He's cutting his own throat. What you people and that idiot know about human nature wouldn't fill a single page.

"Those are real people out there that you're dealing with. They're not B.F. Skinner's rats in a bloody maze. We can't lobotomize or electro-shock the entire world. Though I must admit, we're nearing our goals in drug dependence. What Dutton has tapped in them is pure lightning. They're not going to let go, now that they've had a taste of immortality. Not even with a gun to their heads. This is a new era. Dutton's technology undercuts *everything else*. Next to it, our interests are extremely small potatoes. Don't kid yourselves, gentlemen. Planet Earth is in the middle of a reboot. All bets are off."

It was somewhere north of Wichita that Roxy picked up the NPR news broadcast. When she heard what was going on, she elbowed Sam to wake him. Sam woke the others. A familiar male voice was saying, "...Reported that several units of the California National Guard had been federalized by President Baills last night and ordered to seize the Gillson Electronics facilities in San Jose and a distribution center in Stockton. Gillson Electronics is the American licensee for the Dutton Foxtail. Representatives of the Gillson Corporation could not be reached for comment; however, we have Daniel Dutton himself on the line with us from his residence in New Mexico. What is your response to the President's efforts to negate your work, Mr. Dutton?"

"These actions were not unexpected. When President Forester died, we fully expected some sort of action against us from Baills. He certainly didn't waste any time. It is interesting to note that these efforts have been timed to preempt the public release of our voice technology. Baills has long been known to have links with vested interests that would be anxious to stop the changes this technology is bringing."

"Are you saying, Mr. Dutton, that President Baills was part of a conspiracy to assassinate President Forester?"

"What I'm saying, is that it seems much more than coincidence that action to suppress our technology comes so soon after the death of a President who was very much in support of it."

"And what do you think is to come, Mr. Dutton?"

"I expect the worst. But legal steps are underway to block further illegal action from Baills. The man is not a law unto himself. This country has a Congress to write its laws and a sophisticated judicial system to enforce them. But, in the end, it's the American people who run this country—and they'll make their opinions felt.

Americans will not stand by idly while a renegade administration tramples their freedoms—the freedoms of speech and free association, to name a few. This is not Nazi Germany."

"Do you have any expectations that official action may be taken against you and your family? Of course, we know that you're beyond physical control, but you have living family and friends with you."

"I can't say. It's hard to anticipate what Baills may do now. His moves to suppress the exercise of constitutional rights last night were none too brilliant in their conception. What we're seeing from Baills now are the efforts of a desperate man. They've waited too long to take such action. Actually, it was too late many months ago. Numerous safeguards, with a hundred redundancies, were in place before we undertook public disclosure of this technology. What it boils down to is this— whatever they do, will be for nothing. And by they, I mean Baills and his handlers. The advances this technology is bringing are here to stay. One can slow their progress, but they cannot now be stopped. As for myself and those with me, we expect the worst, and we're ready for it."

"As you've anticipated, Mr. Dutton, Americans are making their views known. I've just been handed a report. It's 2:00 P.M. in Washington, D.C. and sizable demonstrations are underway outside the White House and on Capitol Hill. We have reports that emails and phone calls are flooding the White House and Congress at unprecedented rates—with less than one percent of them in support of Baills. And word has come down that an emergency meeting of the House is underway, reportedly to consider the question of impeachment."

"What can I say," said Dan, "other than what you're reporting from Washington is democracy at its best."

"Excuse me, Mr. Dutton, but I have Claudia Gomez on the line from our affiliate in Albuquerque."

Claudia Gomez began, "Thank you, Bill. I have Jerry Sterling, Daniel Dutton's lead attorney here with me. He's just received some good news. What has happened, Mr. Sterling?"

Jerry responded, "It's about what we expected, Claudia. Judge Howard Blackwell, of the Federal District Court here in Albuquerque, has just ruled that President Baills' ordered closing of six bulletin boards, operated by students at New Mexico junior colleges, is unlawful. The Judge has also issued a broad restraining order that prohibits any action, by any party (including the President), that would have the effect of suppressing activities related to the Dutton technologies. Similar action is expected from the district court in northern California, regarding the seizure of the Gillson facilities there."

"Thank you, Mr. Sterling."

Back in the van, Roxy said, "Dan sure gave 'em hell."

"He did," said Brighton, "But I'm betting it'll encourage our lawless President Baills to take further action against Dan's interests. I'm certain it was Dan's way of spurring public support. In light of the broad public disapproval of Baills' activities, the man will do either of two things—he'll run, or he'll dig in and do as much damage as he can from where he stands."

"What damage can he do?" asked Roxy.

"It all depends upon who's supporting him. I think it's unlikely the military will get involved. Generals know that administrations come and go, but they're in it for life. Even army privates are empowered to disobey illegal orders."

The Brightons, Roxy, and company continued following events on the radio until their arrival in Liberal, Kansas early that evening, where they finally stopped for a meal at a roadside bar and grill. Inside, the bar was packed with customers glued to the screens covering the goings-on in Washington and around the country.

Truly massive demonstrations were underway at all federal offices and military installations across the country. It was estimated that three million people were demonstrating at various locations in Washington D.C. alone, with the largest crowds at the White House and Capitol Hill. Government business had ground to a halt. Traffic blocked all routes into and out of the city; thousands of citizens had just abandoned their vehicles in the middle of the city streets.

It was reported that President Baills had climbed aboard his helicopter on the White House lawn and departed for an unknown destination. His last order had been to call out troops to suppress the demonstrations. No such military action had yet materialized.

In northern California, a Federal District Judge finally ordered the withdrawal of state National Guard units from all Gillson facilities. In addition, he issued a second restraining order, forbidding further interference by President Baills.

Roxy led her party through the crowd to a pool table in a back corner of the establishment. They took seats around several nearby bistro tables and ordered dinner.

Roxy had decided they'd go ahead and look at her maps and begin formulating their strategy for the approach to *Dutton's Warren*, as the Senator called it. Her brother, Steve, started racking the balls at the pool table. Roxy made short work of that idea by spreading out her maps there.

As it turned out, the Duttons were located within the boundaries of a national forest. There was a back route to their place, along a gravel road used by the forest service.

Going northward, the road from Terrero forked—the right led to a mountain recreation area, while the left continued for another eight miles, with the last mile of it along the base of a sheer rock cliff. The road then descended to the valley and the Duttons' place. The survey maps still designated the site and the fork to it—as a restricted area.

Dan had told Roxy that a gate with a camera was still in place at the fork, and could be unlocked remotely from the site.

Chapter 17

Alvin Sheets was apprehensive. A large group of noisy demonstrators had assembled in the drizzle outside his main temple, near Louisville, and had taken to breaking windows in the attached office building. He'd been assured by his contact that neither he, nor his organization, would be implicated with Baills' activities.

Sheets was seated at his ornate desk. "Why on Earth haven't the police done anything about these demonstrations? How do they think we can cope with so many disorderly people? Please, Miss Markham, call the authorities again. I can't carry on the Lord's work when such assaults are ignored by the authorities."

Young, red-headed Lora Markham was at loose ends herself. "I'll call again, Reverend, but it may be that they're tied up with the demonstrations at the government buildings." She started to leave, then turned and said, "I almost forgot. There's a gentleman waiting to see you—a Mr. Wills."

"Wills? I don't believe I know...Oh, yes, I do. Please show him in."

Lora went to the door and ushered in a tall man in his thirties, wearing a damp trench coat and gloves.

Sheets said, "Mr. Wills, for some reason your name just slipped my mind. Won't you take off your wet coat and have a seat?" Sheets offered his hand, but Wills ignored the overture.

Lora left the office and closed the door.

"No, thank you, Reverend. I won't be long." Wills walked over to the large window behind Sheets' desk and looked down on the crowd of demonstrators around the entrance. Others picketed along the road that passed the grand facilities. "It seems you're getting a taste of your own medicine."

"Huh? What do you mean?"

Still looking out the window, Wills replied, "Your door was open. I heard what you told your assistant."

"You what?"

"Americans are none too pleased with the people who fought their deceased President's support of a very popular movement. Now that he's gone, they're infuriated!"

"You sound like you agree with them." Sheets was losing control, his usual self-effacing manner had disappeared.

"In a way, I do." Wills began watching Sheets' reflection in the window.

Sheets turned red with rage. He tried to keep his voice down. "It was you and your people who put me up to it! I could never have sustained the demonstrations, or financed Baills' move against Forester, by my own means. Use of church funds would have been immediately traceable to me."

"You're right, Reverend, on all counts."

In the reflection in the window, Wills watched Sheets turn away; he was going for the phone. Wills reached inside his trench coat and slowly pulled out a semi-automatic pistol fitted with a silencer. He turned, placed the muzzle near the back of Sheets' head and pulled the trigger. There was a muffled thud. Sheets slumped forward onto his desk. A sanguine pool formed quickly as blood flowed copiously from the exit wound in his forehead.

Wills returned the pistol to his coat and leisurely exited the door, taking care not to open it enough for Sheets to be seen from the outer office. He stopped at Lora's desk, she was alone in the outer office, and considered what a waste it would be to have to eliminate the pretty girl as a witness. Wills decided he wouldn't harm her if he could be certain she'd stay out of Sheets' office for a while. He said, "Reverend Sheets asked me to have you hold his calls for fifteen minutes or so. He's reviewing an important document and doesn't want to be disturbed."

Lora smiled, "That's fine. I'm going to sneak out the side door and try to get some lunch. With all the commotion today, I forgot about it. I'll grab something for the Reverend while I'm out."

"If you're leaving now," said Wills, "I'll leave with you—just in case the demonstrators get out of line."

"That's very nice of you. Let me grab my raincoat and umbrella."

About twilight that same evening, a van slowly approached the west ridge gate. The Dutton compound lay in the valley below. A fallen tree blocked the road a hundred feet or so in advance of the closed gate.

The van stopped and a lone man got out. He wore a black jump suit and body armor, a pistol hung from his left shoulder. His ball cap was marked FBI. He climbed over the fallen tree and found that a dozen vehicles—pickups, SUVs, Jeeps, an old school bus, and a dump truck—had been parked barricade-style on the near side of the gate. Several dozen armed men positioned along the barricade, were aiming their weapons threateningly.

The agent looked over his shoulder toward his van. His six men had taken positions behind the tree.

A black man stepped out from the barricade and said, "Have you lost your way?"

The agent said, "I'm FBI Special Agent Bailey. Let us through!"

"How nice, I'm Kingston. You may be FBI, but I'd say today you're S.O.L." Kingston puffed a big cigar, then pulled a remote from his shirt pocket. "This handy little device is the remote trigger for a dozen shaped-charges, all neatly buried beneath those lovely piles of gravel you see along either side of you and your companions."

Bailey and his men looked and found several tons of gravel, as described.

"As you can see," said Kingston, puffing his cigar, "your wisest move might be an honorable retreat."

Bailey turned to his men. "Alright, boys, let's take the gentleman's advice."

Bailey was the last man to return to the van. He hopped in and said, "Okay, so it's Plan B. We'll return to the other side of the ridge and do a hike from the west road."

Dan had warned Roxy about the barricaders' confrontation with the FBI team. It would be after 1:00 A.M. before she and her companions could approach the north end of the valley.

Dan's last report had the FBI team still scaling the far slope of the western ridge, and maybe an hour from its crest. Roxy and company could still beat them to the valley floor, and the night's total lack of moonlight might give them an advantage.

Roxy had extinguished the van's lights for their trek along the west fork of the forest service road. Steve wore night-vision goggles and was riding the van's left running board. The goggles' narrow field of view and short range made traveling dangerous at any significant rate of travel. Four times, they dodged mule deer crossing the road in the dark.

Roxy stopped just before they reached the north end of the valley, and the bridge. Sam got out and launched a hover drone with an infrared camera.

From the bridge, Steve would continue on foot, but not before handing Sam an assault rifle and plenty of clips. Steve himself was carrying a long-range assault rifle and had his old '03 Springfield sniper rifle slung across his back (fittingly, its date of manufacture was December 1941). Both he and Sam wore body armor and carried walkie-talkies. On foot, Steve could see well enough to make his way in the high-altitude starlight. He'd been trained as a long-range sniper and hand-held weapons expert for a special Marine assault unit, and as he liked to add—*with a minor in explosives.*

They crossed the bridge. Recent autumn storms had given rise to the roaring torrent cascading beneath them into the diverted western creek. Only a relative trickle remained to wet the old eastern fork.

The direct route to the Dutton compound, the gravel road going south that lay ahead of them, would have left them like fish in a barrel under any assault from the western ridge. Sam's drone soon confirmed the presence of numerous fallen trees blocking most of the eastern creek bed—much like what Roxy had seen in her survey of four year old satellite images of the area.

With their first-choice alternate route to the Duttons' impassible, Roxy decided they'd head across the somewhat overgrown northern clearing using their only alternative—a badly-rutted dirt road that roughly paralleled the all-but-dry eastern creek. It would be slow-going. As if the rough route weren't enough, the drone's imager had revealed a huge fallen cottonwood blocking the road a hundred yards short of their destination. At that point, they'd resort to the creek bed itself.

Sam left the van, planning to hold back and advance slowly while manning the drone. Steve was going to scout ahead. With the roaring water, they could hardly hear each other speak.

Just as Steve turned to leave, Sam grabbed his arm and said, "Wait! Look at this." Sam pointed toward the drone remote's screen. "There are six...no...seven men on the western ridge." He touched the image. "Six guys, maybe a hundred yards above the creek, one holding back some distance above."

"Okay," Steve replied. "I'll take it easy." He pointed. "I'll advance along the road using the boulders for cover. You hold back here, near the bridge, until I double-click my mic." He reached up to his left shoulder and clicked his walkie's mic button. "Then, you advance to the first of the big boulders. I'll do it again, if I feel you can safely follow past there."

"You got it," said Sam.

"Keep me posted if you see any changes."

"I will."

Roxy turned the van off the gravel and headed along the dirt road in the starlight. A few minutes later, a streak of light shot toward the van from the western ridge, followed by an explosion a dozen yards to the north. The van rocked as shrapnel tore through its side and broke the driver's side window. They'd been the target of a rocket-propelled grenade, an *RPG*.

Roxy and the Brightons were unharmed, but Helen, greatly stressed by their ordeal, began screaming.

Small arms fire echoed across the valley as Steve tore into the ridge with his assault rifle. From positions above, muzzle flashes lit up the dark, looming mass that was the western ridge.

Roxy continued across the clearing somewhat faster than before. It wasn't easy-going with a three-year growth of aspen saplings standing guard the entire length of the bumpy route. Roxy drove over the smallest of them and steered around the larger ones. With a near-miss RPG attack, it certainly wasn't any secret where they were.

Dodging bullets, Steve took a position behind two large boulders on the west side of the road and again cut loose with his assault rifle, drawing fire away from the escaping van. He keyed his walkie and said, "Sam! Fire at the muzzle flashes on the ridge with me, so they can't get off another RPG. Give it some elevation, you're about a hundred yards out."

"You got it." Sam cut into the ridge with his assault rifle. With both of them firing, the guns on the ridge soon fell silent.

Steve flipped down his night goggles. He could see the roaring water immediately west of his position. It would be impossible to cross without exposing himself to their assailants' fire. He shouldered his assault weapon, unslung his sniper rifle, and turned on its night-image scope. He sprinted southward, fifty yards or so, to another huge boulder. Through his goggles, Steve could see Sam still back at the bridge. He double-clicked his mic.

From Steve's walkie earpiece, Sam said, "Those six guys are almost to the creek now. The one above hasn't moved." Steve laid down cover-fire, while Sam sprinted to

Steve's previous position. Again, Sam was on the walkie, "Dig this, Steve—the guys on the ridge, they're headed for a mother-lovin' huge old fallen tree trunk that's bridging the creek. It's actually north of you—like halfway between us."

Again, their assailants cut loose with their assault rifles. Bullets ricocheted off the boulders shielding Steve. Most of the flashes came from positions nearer the base of the ridge, but the guy up the ridge was firing too. Their adversaries hadn't done their homework—they hadn't planned on the creek becoming surging rapids following the recent storms.

Steve raised his goggles, scanned the area with his sniper scope, and spotted the fallen tree bridging the creek. Their adversaries were trying to keep him down, so they could cross first.

Steve keyed his mic. "Sam, can you get a bead on them with your rifle?"

"Sure, Steve...no problem."

"Won't be long before they reach that tree bridging the stream. I want you to take a bead on the first guys to come over and just follow them, don't fire. I'll take care of the others. Got it?"

"Copy," said Sam.

"Good, when I give you the word, let 'em have it."

"Copy. Follow and hold off till you say."

"Roger."

It was several minutes before the men began to show up at the fallen tree. All the while, the man further up the ridge fired on Steve's position. When the six had reached the far end of the tree, Steve aimed his sniper rifle at the muzzle flashes up the ridge. He fired a single round; the distant gun fell silent. It was quality, not quantity, that made one a proficient sniper. The old bolt-action 30-06 was just as deadly in his hands as it had been for Marine snipers back in World War II.

Seconds later, the first two of the six men stepped cautiously onto the natural bridge and began making their way across; one of them was limping badly. When the two had crossed without incident, the remaining four rushed onto the tree all at once. The old rotted tree collapsed, going to pieces beneath them. All four tumbled into the rapids and disappeared.

Steve didn't know if Sam had seen what happened, so he kept silent and moved closer to see what the survivors were up to. He carefully made his way around a big boulder and approached their position. There were four, maybe five, dead already—if he included the guy up the ridge. He'd see what his options were, now that he and

Sam were at more of a tactical advantage. The roaring creek more than covered his voice when he keyed his mic. "Sam, you still got a bead on those two?"

"I do, Steve, but did you see what happened?"

"I did!"

"The two survivors are in a huddle," said Sam. They're not spread out as if they were planning a move."

"Good," said Steve. "I wanna try this without anymore killing. They're not firing, so we probably have an advantage; one of them is wounded. You come in from their north flank, I'll come from the south. Hold off until you hear me click my mic, then come on in. If you don't hear from me, just hold off for further instructions."

"Roger."

Steve continued moving to flank the two. He found he could make them out through his goggles. When he finally got close enough to see what the men were doing, he stopped. One was hunched over the other, who was horizontal on a large rock near the creek. The standing man had a weapon; his companion was motionless. Steve stood up and made his move.

"Okay, guys. Drop your weapons! You, standing—turn around and toss your gun out of reach. Hands behind your head!"

The standing man did as he was told. The other guy had to be unconscious, his bleeding leg needed immediate attention.

"I'll see to your buddy," said Steve. "What's your name?"

"Alvarez. But he's badly hurt!"

"Okay, Alvarez. Kneel down on the ground."

Steve clicked his mic to call Sam in. When Sam arrived, he tied Alvarez' hands and kept him on his knees.

It was a good thing Steve had volunteered for medic training in the corps; the injured man wouldn't make it otherwise. Steve knew first-hand how a man could bleed-out in no time without timely intervention on an arterial wound. It was basically only advanced first-aid, but not knowing had cost him a good Marine buddy before he made a point of learning what to do and why.

A Marine battlefield surgeon, Major Chapman, had boiled the subject down to its basics for Steve. "Keeping a cool head is the biggest factor in battlefield medicine. After that, it's stopping the loss of blood that comes with battlefield trauma. Your buddy can lose just so much before he's doomed—it's up to you to make the difference."

From their walkies came Roxy's voice, "Steve? Sam? Are you guys all right? We're almost to the creek bed, but we're basically stuck. We're going to need some help just clearing the way."

Steve grabbed his walkie with his spare hand; he had the heel of his right hand pressing hard against a femoral pressure point protecting the man's wounded thigh. "We're okay. But we've got two prisoners. One has a nasty arterial wound—he's lost a lot of blood. If I take my hand off his artery, he's not gonna make it."

"Dan's been watching you," said Roxy. "He took off to check the ridge for any more bad guys. He should be back soon."

"Sounds good. I was gonna ask if he could do just that." Steve let go of his walkie button and said, "Sam, why don't you poke around and see if they brought any other gear. We got here just in time. This man has almost bled-out."

"You got it."

To Alvarez, Steve said, "You made the right choice, man. You made the difference between your buddy here having a chance or winding up a corpse."

"He's my friend. He'd have done the same for me."

A few minutes later, Sam had found quite a cache. "What do you think, Steve? They were behind that boulder."

"You struck it rich, Sam. An RPG and four grenades! Can you keep an eye on Alvarez? His buddy here is in shock from loss of blood."

Roxy came back on the walkie, "Dan says the area's clear, Steve. No one within fifteen miles of us except for a dead man up the ridge and the twenty-six guys manning the barricade. He found radio-jamming equipment near the top of the ridge. That explains the trouble they've been having with the site's cellular repeater. Dan says the doc brought some plasma—six pints—and a case of lactated Ringer's solution. But *no* whole blood."

"Thanks, Sis. We'll need them."

"Listen, Steve," continued Roxy. "Since it's basically safe on the main road now—if your injured man is that serious, maybe someone can get another vehicle up to you quicker from the compound. We've got this van between a rock and a hard place just now. It'll take some work to get us out. I'd hate for us to lose your patient when we could speed things up."

"Damn, Roxy, you're right. This *isn't* a battlefield anymore!"

Minutes later, Sarah arrived in their Jeep. Steve would continue treating the wounded man as they headed for the compound.

Roxy made it to the back entrance platform on foot, just as Sarah's Jeep arrived with Steve, Alvarez, and their patient.

Roxy said, "Hello, Mrs. Dutton."

"Hi, Roxy. It's great to finally meet you."

"Hey, Sis," said Steve. "If you can take over the pressure on this guy's leg, I'll go help with the van. Sam should be there by now."

Roxy climbed into the back of the open Jeep and said, "Just a sec...okay, I've got it, Steve." She checked the man's pupils and carotid pulse, then smiled and said, "You done good, little brother. You saved this guy's life."

David Alvarez offered to help, saying that it didn't make sense to continue opposing good people who were only trying to do the right thing. He left with Steve to help retrieve the van.

Senator Brighton and Sam (who'd made it over to the van on foot) were already trying to clear the way when Steve and David arrived. And Roxy was right, there were plenty of obstacles along the creek bed. With the help of all hands, they managed to move three rotting trees out of the way—two required a tow chain hooked to the van's bumper.

The main surface entrance to the underground site was immense. The three-inch-thick doors were eighteen feet high and big enough to accommodate huge mining equipment, helicopters, and heavy trucks.

The entrance was situated atop a massive concrete platform some fifteen feet above the creek bed. A broad ramp led from the creek to the platform, while a second led from the platform to the clearing and the domed silo building above.

With the majority of the creek's flow diverted across to the western side of the valley, there was little chance that flooding could ever reach the level of the door platform.

Dawn was still an hour away when Steve drove the van up the ramp to the platform and the massive doors. David Alvarez and Sam made it up on foot.

The doors moaned as powerful electric motors hummed to life. Ever so slowly, the hulking masses began sliding apart. When they'd separated, a dim red light lit the space beyond.

When the doors had opened sufficiently, a woman stepped through the space followed by a young girl.

The Senator told his wife, "Helen, that's Sarah Dutton and their daughter, Jessica. I'm getting out." He slid open the van's side door and stepped out.

Helen Brighton said, "Wait! I'm coming too, Bill," and stepped out behind him.

"Hi, Sarah," said Senator Brighton.

Warmly, Sarah said, "Hello, Senator," and gave him a big hug. "I'm so glad you made it safely." She turned to Mrs. Brighton. "Helen?"

"Yes." The two of them hugged a long, understanding hug. Helen broke into tears. "Thank you for having us come to stay with you, Sarah. It's been such an ordeal. Five men died tonight trying to kill us, after President Forester and Linda, and all of those innocent people on the plane. How can anyone be so cold-blooded as to do these things?"

"Maybe we should ask Morgan Baills," replied Sarah. To the young men, she said, "I know you're all done in from your trip, but if there's any possibility..." She pointed toward the dome, "We've got three trailers of provisions behind the silo building. Dan's afraid if we don't get them underground soon, they'll be destroyed."

David Alvarez was understandably ill at ease when he said, "I know all of you have more than enough reason not to trust me, but I'm convinced you're good people. You've put yourselves out to save my friend's life; that means a great deal to me, after what we were up to tonight. I'd be glad to help you in any way I can. But I won't be offended if you just decide to lock me up somewhere."

Steve spoke up, "Sam and I can move your trailers, Mrs. Dutton." He patted David's shoulder. "With David willing to help, you've got three volunteers."

Sarah smiled and looked relieved. "Thank you. We have a semi-tractor. The trailers will have to be taken down through this door. The doctor and I drove the cars and pickup down this afternoon. The semi-tractor is up in the silo building. Neither of us were up to handling a semi-rig and trailers. And Jerry isn't back from Santa Fe, he's still at the hospital with Marsha Gambles."

"It's not a problem, ma'am," said Sam. "I drove a semi-rig for two years, earning money for college. We'll have them tucked away in no time."

Steve drove all of them down into Dutton's Warren and to the living quarters. Their patient, Michael Williams, was already in surgery with Dr. Smithson and Roxy in their makeshift operating room. Thirty minutes later, the worst of it was over. It turned out that they needed whole blood. David Alvarez was the same blood type, so he stayed back to help his friend.

In the meantime, Sarah had escorted Steve and Sam up the elevator and explained the lockouts and controls for the silo building's surface doors. Once the guys had hitched up the tractor to the first of the trailers, she made her way down the ramp to the surface tunnel doors and opened them again. Dan stood guard while they hauled the provisions inside.

When the trailers were snug in a corner of the storehouse cavern, the young men met several of the barricaders at the compound gate and loaded the Jeep with arms and equipment commandeered from the FBI team's van (which Dan had discovered earlier, while scouting the vicinity).

Steve turned the switch lockout key and pushed the stairway hatch button. "You know, Sam, I'll be training you and Roxy in how to use the RPG you found tonight. My big sister could come in handy in a pinch, she's certainly got the nerve."

Chapter 18

Agent Michael Williams was doing well the morning after his surgery. He and David Alvarez, both basically FBI rookies, had seen their first real action the night before.

Dan decided it made good sense to question them separately, starting with Williams. Alvarez was given his own room, but no further access to their domain; he admitted he'd probably not have been quite as trusting had the tables been turned.

Senator Brighton and Roxy sat in Williams' room while he wolfed down his breakfast. "How are you doing today, Michael?" asked Dan from the foxtail in Roxy's shirt pocket.

"I'm doing pretty well just now, thanks," replied Williams. "But I came close to needing your interface myself last night. I was all but gone, until someone pulled me back."

"You almost bled to death."

"I thought I had. It was like I was watching a movie, with my dead body laid out on that rock. Wish you'd been doing this when I was a kid."

"Why is that?"

"My mother died right in front of me, when I was nine. I was all alone in the house, I dialed 911."

"I'm sorry, Michael, it's not easy losing a parent, but it's especially hard for a child."

"I had no dad. My grandparents wound up raising me. One thing though, Mom, she..." Michael began tearing up. "My mom, she came back that same night to say goodbye. It was her, I saw her. Honestly. I could even smell her favorite perfume. And then, for years afterward, there'd be times I'd smell it again, when I was alone. I'd just knew she was checking on me."

"I'm sorry, Michael. I wish we'd had the technology then. You'd be surprised how many people have similar experiences. It's just part of being human that such things occur."

"It would have been wonderful to have had her in my life growing up," said Michael. "Even just as you are here, Mr. Dutton. That would have been enough. That would have made all the difference, just being able to talk with her, share my life with her. The truth is, last night made me reevaluate my purposes in being here; being that close to death in the world you've given us. I don't think I could bring myself to doing it again."

"Thank you, Michael. And you're here, recovering, because some very good people cared enough to save a man in trouble, regardless of his efforts to harm them. You could have bled to death if Steve, Roxy, and the doctor weren't good people."

"I know," said Michael. "I'm sorry for my part in this. I'd be dead if I couldn't trust you."

"And so would my wife and I," said Senator Brighton. "Daniel is everything he claims to be, Michael. Our world will be a much better place for all of us, and for posterity, because of what he's doing."

"I'm seeing that, Senator," said Michael. "I know it's true."

Dan asked, "Can we talk about what brought you here last night?"

"Certainly, I owe you that."

"When did you arrive in the area?"

"We arrived just about dusk yesterday evening, and immediately had a confrontation with the people at your barricade on the western ridge. By then I'd been having my doubts about what I'd become a part of. The confrontation amounted to a validation of those doubts. To find that you had regular citizens willing to lay it on the line, supporters who were willing to stand up to the establishment, to us, in your defense."

"They're tough-minded people. I'm proud of them. And of you, for daring to take the bigger view of what all this can mean for the future."

Michael said, "And who could ever have dreamt of such a world?"

Roxy replied, "Dan did, in his last novel. About four years ago."

Senator Brighton added, "There was a philosopher who said, 'It's the artist who sees the future first.'"

"Hadn't thought of it that way, Senator." said Roxy, smiling. "But it's true."

"It is," said Dan. "But getting back to our current situation, Michael. Could you tell me where your team was previously, before you came here?"

"D.C."

"Where your team forced its way into Senator Brighton's residence?"

"That's right, sir," admitted Michael.

"And what was it you were told, to justify your attack here last night?"

"We were told that the Senator and the Duttons were involved in a conspiracy that resulted in President Forester's death."

"Okay, Michael, help me with this. With all of the agents available for FBI operations, if you were being told the truth, why would it make sense to rush the same agents from D.C. to New Mexico? Don't they have FBI personnel out here?"

"They do. But we were told we were a specially-picked group."

"Uh-huh. I think you were, but sadly, not for the reasons you assumed. Is this particular conspiracy theory generally held throughout the security community? If there's any truth to it, why hasn't everyone in the community been brought into what you and your people intended to do here last night?"

Michael wrinkled his brow. "I can't say for sure, sir. I know it was believed there were several others involved. Maybe my superiors suspected there were conspirators in the security community as well."

"Perhaps. What were you told about Director Simmons' death?"

"What do you mean, *what was I told?*"

"Then I assume you were told it was an accident."

"We were. It was, wasn't it?"

"Sadly, no. You've been misled, Michael. Director Simmons had just been informed of a conspiracy from within the administration, that same morning. He was silenced to keep him from spoiling the conspirator's plans. Simmons had been informed by President Forester himself, who had learned about it from Senator Brighton."

Michael was visibly shaken. He shivered as a chill ran up his spine. "Director Simmons was murdered? I met him, the day I was sworn in. He's...he was a good man."

"He is," said Dan. "Director Simmons was moving to prevent President Forester's assassination when he was killed."

Williams shook his head, devastated. "Who? Who in the administration was involved? I haven't heard anything about administration complicity."

"Baills," said Dan.

"President Baills? You've gotta be kidding."

"Isn't it obvious from Baills' actions—blocking interface distribution and the bulletin boards—that he had Forester killed? Killed so he could shut us down and take over the administration? Haven't you heard about the public uproar over Baills' actions against us? Washington has been paralyzed by demonstrations. The people want Baills out of office. Even the courts are working against him; they've ordered him to cease all action against us. And yet, here you are."

"I had no idea. We'd been ordered to come straight here, stopping only for fuel. They'd packed ice chests with food, so we wouldn't have to stop to eat."

"I'll bet you didn't have a radio, either."

"You're right. Or our phones." Michael was getting the picture. "Our team leader told us the van radio wasn't working, so no one even tried it. Now that you mention it...he didn't even want us buying a newspaper. In fact, he always paid for the gas. We stayed in the van...except for using the john."

"Your team leader, Bailey, didn't make it last night. He'd gone rogue, he was involved in Simmons' death. He'd been bought.

"Bailey killed Director Simmons?"

"Might as well have," said Dan. "Bailey was one of many associate-deputies to the Director. After Simmons' death, Bailey managed a bogus recall of the agents assigned to us at the President's request. And then he just fell off the Bureau's radar—masquerading as your team leader to further Baills' program to undermine our position. The conspiracy's success required keeping their operation very small. You and your team were only the latest of their dupes—in on it, but not."

"How do you? Who told you all this?"

"He did."

"Bailey?"

"We found his body up the ridge this morning; I've learned most of this directly from him. He's had some major second thoughts since, regarding his crimes and motivations. He'd let you and your buddies take the big risks, you were expendable."

Michael looked away, lost in thought, and finally said, "You'll have to excuse me. I have friends who've spoken with the dead, but hearing one dead man share what he's learned from another is quite a leap for me."

"I appreciate your uneasiness with these circumstances, Michael," said Dan. "Take your time."

"What you've said explains a lot. Even with him being my senior, I never really trusted the man. Can't say I'm surprised he was someone who'd let himself be bought, bought to sell out our President, and Director Simmons."

"And almost five dozen other innocent souls."

"What a scum bag. How do people do such things?"

"Greed and the promise of vast unearned wealth, in trade for whatever honor a man might once have possessed."

"It's amazing that a few people could do such great harm."

"In total, there have probably been no more than six or eight federal employees knowingly involved, from *Air Force One* through today. Baills and his minions care nothing for what's right in the world; it's all about money and power. And beyond them, there's an outside agenda we may never fully understand."

"So this conspiracy originates from outside the government?"

"It does."

"I wish I'd been brighter than to follow Bailey blindly, brighter than to be part of furthering their aims here last night."

"If only Bailey had known we had an expert Marine Corps sniper on our side. It's a good thing for you that that sniper, Steve, is also a medic."

That set Michael off, "Now hold it right there—a Marine? You're saying it was Steve who saved my life on that rock? And—and Steve's a Marine?"

"He is," answered Roxy. "Steve mustered out just two weeks ago."

"Damn!" said Michael. "I mustered out two years back. No way I'd have had any part in this if I'd known I was aiming at a fellow Marine." Michael smiled. "I should have known by his tactics. What was his unit?"

"You can ask him yourself," said Roxy. He's in the next room. Steve was duty-bound that he—that we—were going to save you. It was Steve who got to you first. He'd lost friends in battle before he knew what to do. He wasn't going to lose you too."

"Damn! I'd like to thank him. Maybe over a beer," said Michael, smiling. "Hey, dig that—a Marine saved my life."

Dan said, "I think we can arrange that, and the beer. And we'll give you a chance to catch up on the news about Baills and the demonstrations. We even have one of your colleagues from the FBI here with us. Pete refused an illegal order to be recalled from his posting here, a posting ordered by President Forester himself. Christ, I can do better than that. I can let you speak with President Forester."

A week later, when Williams could travel, he and Alvarez made their way to Santa Fe. Before leaving, Michael offered Dan his assistance with any and all future circumstances, saying they'd made him feel like he still had a family.

Five days were enough for Marsha. With hospital food and being roused in the middle of the night to take medication she didn't need, she had ample incentive to make a quick exit. Her pretty face was still bruised, but her bruises were yellowing and would soon disappear. Even if her doctor had insisted on another two days, Marsha checked out at 10:00 A.M. She felt safe enough, with Baills' recent setbacks and Sheets' death, to say good-bye to the hospital.

Without a doubt, several of the biggest stories in all of history had occurred while she was on her back. She wasn't going to let more history get by without her. Besides, she was certain the Duttons had need of her now, in perhaps their most critical hour.

Once her boss understood Marsha's plans, he put a network helicopter and pilot at her disposal. That morning, Jerry was in Albuquerque getting things from her apartment and filling her prescriptions. The chopper was going to meet them at the hospital in Santa Fe, then they'd fly to the Dutton's compound. Dan thought Marsha should stay with them and the rest of their contingent, which now included the Brightons, Dr. Smithson, the Foresters, Judy, and Wally Harris.

Steve and Sam were on body detail. Agent Bailey's body had been retrieved first, up the ridge, the day before—at which time they'd also destroyed the jamming equipment Dan had found.

Locating the bodies down the creek had proven no easy task. Two had been washed over a falls a half-mile downstream. All had been placed in body bags and loaded into the back of Roxy's van.

It wasn't the first time Steve had killed a man in action, but he still felt guilty. His dad had always said, "The true resolution to any conflict is always and only *communication.* No sane man resorts to bullets when he can look his opponent in the eye." Steve wasn't happy about any of it, but the survival of the group came first. What the Duttons were doing was bigger than anything he'd ever been a part of, even the Corps.

Chapter 19

A young nurse wheeled Marsha out of the E.R. entrance and toward the waiting helicopter. Jerry stepped down from the aircraft and ducked the whirling blades; he nodded and took over for the nurse. Raising his voice to be heard, Jerry said, "Hi, sweetie. Your producer just called, the crew is on its way up to Dan's for tonight's broadcast. I hope you're feeling up to this."

Jerry locked the wheelchair's wheels, helped Marsha to her feet, and they ducked inside the chopper. "I'm good today, Jerry. This is what I should be doing—interviewing Forester. I've missed too much, and so has my audience."

"You've been out of the loop, but I know you'll enjoy your new digs up in the mountains."

"My what?"

"Dan had an apartment built for you."

"An apartment?"

"Plus a studio of your own—lighting, green screen, cameras, dedicated satellite-link and all. Barney has been up several times supervising the technical stuff."

"Wow! That's so sweet. Sarah never said anything. What a stinker."

Jerry grinned and said, "My place is just down the hall."

Kermit Weller was not a happy man. Nothing had gone as he'd expected—that idiot, Baills, had held him off too long. Besides that, he'd been *a* fool for an idiot in the first place, to go along with that hare-brained scheme in return for Baills' pie-in-the-sky promises. He felt as gullible as dead Brad Weston—thinking his betrayal of their President would only cost him a stomach ache and a trip to the emergency room.

So now, Baills was in Colorado, waiting it out while the House of Representatives considered impeachment.

Kermit was convinced it was just a matter of time before they caught up with him. He could feel it coming. If he'd been smart, he'd have been long gone. The thing was, where could he go that they wouldn't want to string him up?

The vidphone rang. Kermit flinched. He hated answering the damned thing anymore. Oh, well. He hit the answer key. The video image formed, but no one was there, just a U.S. map on a wall. Uh-oh, he thought, here it comes.

"Kermit."

Kermit swallowed hard. "Yes."

"This is Wally Harris."

Bright and cheerful, with makeup over her bruises, Marsha looked into the camera and smiled. When the red light on Barney's camera lit up, and her producer gave her the signal, she said, "Hello. I'm Marsha Gambles and this is a *Sunday Special Report*. Tonight, we have a most important interview, with President Theodore Rice Forester. We're coming to you from the Dutton residence. We're in their living room, looking out at a beautiful New Mexico sunset through the big-screen monitor that is their living room window." The pick-up, normally panning about the property, was fixed westward. The dark, jagged bulk of the Sangre De Cristo Mountains was silhouetted against blazing hues of red and gold.

"President Forester will be speaking with us using one of the Dutton foxtails. This same voice interface will begin its release to the public tomorrow—quantities will be limited, but we're told that the supply should catch up with demand in the U.S. by New Year's. President Forester, thank you for agreeing to this interview."

"You're certainly welcome, Marsha." The screen cut to an image of a speaker sitting beside a foxtail interface. That image dissolved to a file photo of Forester and would dissolve through a collection of images from his professional career for the television audience to view while the President was speaking.

"What would you like to tell us, Sir?"

"First," said Forester, "I'd like to say, 'Hello. Yes. It's me! Through the efforts of my friends, I'm here to share my experiences and thoughts with you. Also my hopes for our future."

"A great many lives have been lost in the last week. Marsha Gambles, herself, was injured in an effort to prevent any of us from doing precisely what I'm doing this evening. My wife and I, and fifty-five others, died in the crash of *Air Force One* last Wednesday. Charles Simmons, our FBI Director, died less than an hour earlier. He was murdered just as he was trying to prevent an assassination attempt uncovered by Daniel Dutton, an act with the sole objective of preventing the dissemination and proliferation of Dutton's technology."

Marsha asked, "President Forester, can you say who was involved in the conspiracy?"

"We knew of the activities and plans of two of the individuals before the assassination. Since then, a third has come forward—Secret Service Director Kermit Weller. Weller has revealed a fourth—Arthur Bailey, an associate-deputy director with the FBI, now deceased.

"The conspirators known to be involved before my death were Morgan Baills and Alvin Sheets. As you know, Reverend Sheets was murdered in his office in Louisville last Friday. President Baills, as your viewers are probably aware, is under house arrest at his vacation home in the Colorado Rockies, and is the subject of a House investigation.

"Director Weller came forward after being confronted with evidence provided by an individual who died with me last Wednesday.

"As we speak, three of the four named conspirators are testifying before a federal grand jury. Physical evidence recovered from the aircraft wreckage led investigators to believe that someone with access to the plane had planted devices onboard. Director Weller has substantiated that theory and is supplying details to the grand jury. Three others, all military officers, are also being indicted."

"Do we know anything more," asked Marsha, "about the group that attacked Senator Brighton and his traveling companions Saturday?"

"We do. Originally from Weller, and later substantiated by the deceased Agent Bailey. They were a group of inexperienced FBI agents, led by Bailey, on what they believed to be a legitimate mission against the conspirators behind Wednesday's assassination. We now know for a fact that Bailey was the only Bureau agent involved in the conspiracy.

"Interestingly, two FBI agents assigned to the Duttons were unlawfully recalled by Bailey last Tuesday night, the night before the assassination. One of the two refused to obey the illegal order, and remains at his post with the Duttons."

Marsha asked, "What are your plans for the future, President Forester?"

"I'd like to continue where I left off last Wednesday. I know my funeral was just yesterday, but that means little or nothing now. I want to continue as President for the remainder of my term, and I want to run for a second term. I see no reason that I shouldn't be able to resume my duties. There's certainly no chance of my dying while in office."

Marsha smiled. "Do you think the American people would support such an unprecedented arrangement?"

"In light of today's realities, I feel they would. Nothing has changed regarding my ability to govern. Personally, I would prefer having a President in my state. I can tell you, first-hand, that it's extremely difficult to pull the wool over the eyes of one aware of another's thoughts. I know, with a great deal of certainty, that a leader without physical limitations could be a great deal more responsive to the needs of his countrymen.

"The American people voted me into office because they wanted me for the job. As far as I've been able to tell, they've been pretty happy with my performance.

"Perhaps the most important reason I feel I should continue is that while we're adjusting to a completely new set of realities, our country needs someone at the helm with broad experience in both states of existence, and in the office of President. There's no one else standing by who meets all of these qualifications.

"Once this technology is widely available, the entire fabric of our culture is going to change for the better. We don't want a country or a culture with two classes of citizens. Our nation's Bill of Rights, and the laws by which we coexist as living men and women, must encompass these new realities. They must provide our newly-recovered citizens the same rights as the living. Besides, we need them. Just think of what we'll regain in lost talent and skill alone.

"To put it succinctly: Our loss today, is future gain. It is a basic truth. And now we can plan for it.

"I feel the biggest changes will come with the end of our strictly mortal view of life. The hallmarks of that mortal view are our history of violence and greed, that more than anything define our world, along with a purely mortal preoccupation with the accumulation of wealth and the domination of others. These symptoms will fall away as we move forward knowingly as the immortals we have always been.

"Why should men and women work a lifetime just to hand the fruits of their labors to others, when they need them themselves? Bodies do wear out, like all other machinery. The apparency has been that the failure of our personal, biological vehicles is the end of us. We know today, without equivocation, that that is not the case. In time, all of you will intimately grasp the necessity of this legal redefinition of citizenship and basic rights.

"My disembodied brethren and I, and your future selves, are and will be every bit as much deserving of rights as the living."

Chapter 20

Morgan Baills had become a little man in a corner. Sitting in his vacation home in the Colorado Rockies, under house arrest, he'd finally grasped the truth of it—he'd done nothing wrong. Certainly the timing had been less than perfect, but events had forced the timing on him. No, somewhere Weller and his people had screwed it up. Even Sheets had let him down. That dim-witted simp had gotten himself killed, hadn't he? Now, Weller himself had turned on Baills, and people were in a fuss over what Weller and his men had done.

Why they wanted anything from him, Baills couldn't say. Certainly he'd had some inkling of what Weller had been up to, but surely that's not the same as being guilty of conspiracy against the President. He'd had nothing to do with the details or execution of the project, though he'd agreed it was necessary. If anyone was responsible, it was Sheets. It had been his money. Weller could tell them that. Yes, it was their fault— Sheets and Weller. And now Weller wanted to pull him down because he couldn't face it alone.

As far as the executive orders went, Baills had had no choice. He had to act quickly to protect the country and even the world from themselves, in their headlong rush to destruction. The Devil had to be denied the use of such tools. Besides, it wouldn't do to have disembodied spirits sticking their noses into everything and blabbing all to everyone over Dutton's accursed inventions. It just wouldn't do. One had to act.

Doctors Palkin, Silva, and Banning sat together again, this time over sherry at a different table.

"Bails has really made an awful mess of this entire affair," said Palkin. "If we'd left Sheets around to point a finger, it could have been much worse. With Forester last night, and the news this morning, I'm truly disappointed. This does absolutely nothing to help our position."

"You're still the master of the understatement, Leonard," added Teller Banning. "What position? That cretin, Bails, has left us no position at all."

"Are there no options left to us?" asked Dimitri Silva.

Banning said, "We might slow the process down enough to allow us time to formulate some way to profit from the new circumstances. Who knows, maybe there's some other way to turn this to our advantage. Counseling the newly-dead perhaps, on how best to make the adjustment to their new circumstances."

"Surely you're joking," said Palkin.

Banning laughed. "You can bet that very soon the American entrepreneurial impulse will contrive innumerable ways to make money out of all of this. Mark my words, the banking and insurance industries will be among the first."

"So, what do you propose we do?" asked Palkin.

"Well. Let's just think about it," said Banning. "The less coherent the leadership during the onset of broad public use of this technology, the better. If we can disrupt Dutton's organization, or even shut it down, we might just wind up running this show. We could just fill the vacuum."

Silva added, "You say all we need to do is upset his organization or close it down. How do you propose we shut down an organization run by a dead man? There's no way we can get at him."

"It's simple, Dimitri," said Banning. "Think about it. We do it by changing the status of the living members of his organization. Eliminate them. Certainly surviving death is a major breakthrough in understanding Man. But these disembodied need the support of the living to be able to create any real effect in the living world. Convert Dutton's living facilitators and you've essentially put him out of business, for the time being at least. And that most certainly includes Senator Brighton."

"They're his foundation," Banning continued. Without them, he's just another of the disembodied jabbering out of an interface. And there will soon be millions, thanks to Dutton's enterprise in making the technology available. Let's just make his efforts work against him. What we need to do is win. It doesn't matter how. If we can't eliminate the technology, we do what we can to control it. Then *we* would become the facilitators to the dead—at a profit, of course."

"And how do we manage depriving Dutton of his living associates?" asked Palkin.

"Right now, it would be relatively easy," said Banning. "They're all in that rabbit hole of his."

"So?" said Silva. "That hole is proofed against all but a nuclear assault."

"True, but with stealth, and an ace up our sleeve, a great deal can be accomplished."

Chapter 21

It was a late September evening, and it was getting cool in the mountains. Jessica was in the woods with Terra, in their favorite spot. After playing hard in a small clearing between the aspens and the squat pinion pines at the foot of the eastern ridge, they laid down exhausted on a bed of yellow aspen leaves to rest. Jessica gazed upward and watched the clouds and soaring hawks and vultures. Terra lay beside her, tracking a black-tailed jackrabbit with her alert brown eyes and broken-tipped collie ears. Jessica's eyes closed of their own accord, and she fell asleep.

When she awoke, it was dark.

From high over the clearing came a sound like a dull, repetitive wooosh, coming closer and closer. The longer she listened, the more it seemed to come from two separate points, rapidly descending toward the open ground north and south of the compound. Terra stood up and barked.

Then the thought struck Jessica—the tunnel door. She'd left it open.

Jessica jumped to her feet. She and Terra made their way through the moonlit woods as quickly as possible. She stopped a moment and strained to hear the sounds again.

They'd stopped.

A chill ran up Jessica's spine. They bolted across the creek bed in the stark moonlight. By the time they'd scaled the back ramp, they were both panting heavily.

The door was as she'd left it, but something was wrong. A figure stood in the doorway, eerily silhouetted in the red light. Terra barked.

Someone grabbed Jessica from behind. A gloved hand covered her mouth. Terra tore into the man's leg and he yelled in pain. *"Got ver dommen, hond!"* The man kicked at the collie. Terra came back for more.

Jessica pulled the hand away from her mouth. "Terra! Run! Run! Go to the barricade and get help. Now! Run!"

Jessica reached out for her father. The man hit her hard and she slumped to the ground.

Terra hesitated, she wanted to stay and protect Jessica. The man pulled a weapon from his shoulder. A rapid series of flashes lit up the dark as he fired at the collie. Unscathed, Terra deftly, and at full gait, turned and disappeared into the dark shadows.

Inside, Dan felt Jessica's cry. He dropped what he was doing, and in a blink was outside the tunnel doors. Jessica lay still, but alive on the concrete platform. Just a few steps away lay Pete—dead. In the clearing were two large black helicopters, one at either end of the compound. Neither had any markings. Visible in the red light beyond the huge steel doors were a dozen armed men in full body armor, wearing gas masks.

But there was someone else out on the platform, someone Dan almost missed. Warner—a dead man like himself, standing off to one side, just watching.

Dan moved from the surface to the base of the spiraling tunnel. There were voices and the rumble of distant boots coming his way. He moved toward them and found a squad of armed men in gas masks descending at double-time, each with a metal canister slung at his side. They had two city blocks yet to go.

Dan jumped back to their quarters and grabbed the interface in the living room. Everyone was up and about their business. "All of you, stop! Stop what you're doing! Men are on their way down here with weapons and poison gas. Jessica has been hurt...but she's alive."

Sarah screamed, "Jessica! We've got to help Jessica."

"Not now, Sarah. These men are here to kill everyone. Listen to me, all of you— make certain you have a working interface. Hold them up, show me." All but Margaret Brighton held up their interface. "Sarah, please get one for Margaret."

"Sure, Dan."

"Steve."

"Yes, sir."

"Close the seals leading from the silo bay. Close all the seals! I don't want them getting past the silos. And shut off the ventilators and retract the stacks. Sam, you go with him. Then get your arms and gear, including gas masks, and do what you can to keep these guys in the silo bay."

"Yes, sir," said Steve. He and Sam turned and sprinted out of the room in the direction of the silos. They stopped in the adjacent hallway, where Steve opened an electrical panel and threw several switches. The air fell still and a rumbling began as the stack covers were retracted into their hardened cradles.

Out on the surface, an armed man lobbed a gas canister toward one of the retracting ventilation stacks in the clearing. The air intake clanked into its sealed cradle an instant before the canister bounced off and rolled into the nearby pinion thicket, spewing its poison harmlessly to the wind.

Back inside, Dan said, "Roxy! Follow Steve and get your gear in the armory across the hall. I want you in protective gear, and a gas mask, and armed to the teeth just inside the quarters seal. And keep a medical kit with you."

"Okay, Dan," said Roxy with serious intent, then she sprinted down the hall after her brother.

Out in the silo bay, the quarters seal began sliding shut. Across the cavern, the first of the armed men reached the bottom and fired at the doors as the mechanism sped to close the space between them. Their bullets ricocheted off, to no effect.

Back in their quarters, Dan was still giving orders, "I need everyone's help. Jerry. Senator. Go to the armory and get yourselves armed. Jerry, I need you with Steve and Sam."

"Aye, Captain," said Jerry, as he turned to Marsha and gave her a quick kiss. He and the senator quickly left the room.

"Joseph, please try to stay close to treat the injured. Sarah and Marsha, I need you armed and in flack jackets and gas masks. Walkie-talkies work only hit-and-miss down here, so I'm going to ask Judy to keep in touch with everyone and keep me informed through our interfaces. Is that okay with you, Judy?"

Judy was across the room. Dan didn't need an interface with her. He felt, rather than heard her response. "Anything for my family," said Judy.

"Thanks. Just roam around and follow the action. Let me know what's going on and if anyone needs anything."

Judy nodded and was gone.

"Wally? Would you go up and stay with Jessica?"

Wally Harris was nearby, "Yes, sir."

"I don't have a way of getting anyone up there to move her to a safer location just now."

"I'll stay close," said Wally, "and I'll keep you informed." Wally disappeared.

"Ted, while I'm outside, you and Linda can poke around and help keep me abreast of what's going on below ground."

"All right, Dan," said Ted. "We'll stay in touch."

"Thanks, we'll be seeing some action here any second now."

There was an explosion on the surface. The whole cavern shook. Dan remembered the satellite dish, and activated the office vidphone. No response. They'd already cut them off from the satellite network.

Dan remarked, "Like I said." And was gone.

He arrived on the surface near the antenna, or rather where it should have been. It was gone. The debris from the explosion was raining down all around him. Again, Dan noticed the big black choppers in the moonlight. He'd let himself become too distracted; this never should have happened.

Then Dan remembered the barricade—Kingston had an interface. He jumped to the barricade and found four of the vehicles, already loaded with armed men, heading down the mountain road to the compound. Terra was running out ahead of them, leading the way.

Dan found Kingston's truck. He grabbed Kingston's device and said, "This is Daniel Dutton. Obviously, we're under attack! They've entered the site through the tunnel doors and they're heavily armed. Do not enter the underground! They intend to gas us. I'll open the gates to the compound and let you into the silo building—at least you'll have cover there, and weapons."

Kingston said, "Whatever you need, Daniel, we will do."

Dan jumped behind the silo building, where he found three of the assailants running down the incline toward the tunnel doors. The moon was just above the eastern ridge. Dan began pulling together a bright, palpable image—much like he'd done at the first interview with Marsha. Out of nowhere, an apparition appeared before the men—stopping them in their tracks. The black-cloaked figure of the Grim Reaper, with burning red eyes, confronted the three men. Long skeletal fingers gripped the handle of his blood-smeared scythe. The Reaper lunged toward them, howling and swinging the blade. They backed away and opened fire on the specter.

When he laughed and lunged again, they turned, screaming, and bolted. One of them tripped; the others tumbled over him in the dark. They scrambled to their feet. Dan chased them theatrically up the incline and into the clearing.

There were now fourteen raiders inside. Outside the seal between the quarters and the silo bay, two of them were setting plastic explosives. Steve, Sam, and Jerry, armed and wearing their protective gear, cautiously left the quarters through the engineering seal at the south end of the silo cavern. They took up a position on the cavern floor out toward the concrete works at the base of the missile cradles. Fortunately, there was some light from the fixtures across the cavern—Steve's night-vision goggles wouldn't fit over his gas mask.

Pale green smoke clung to the floor in all directions—its source, two canisters still spewing near the tunnel entrance north of them. Thankfully, the agent they released wasn't active through skin contact; they weren't suffering any ill-effects.

Steve flicked on the night scope on his sniper rifle. He took aim at one of the two men near the quarters seal. His shot rang out and the man slumped to the ground. Then another, the second man followed the first before he could arm the pouch of explosives.

From a position above the three of them, muzzles flashed as silenced automatic weapons were fired. The bullets missed them, ricocheting off the concrete floor and striking the wall beyond. Two men were on the lower landing halfway up the silo. Steve shifted the muzzle of his rifle toward the spot and took aim. A shot rang out and one of the men fell. They heard his muffled screams through the man's gas mask, until the instant he hit the hard concrete floor eighty feet below. The second man ducked into the elevator and headed for the upper landing.

Four more of the raiders ran toward the quarters seal from the entrance to the inclined tunnel. When they'd reached their objective, two of them laid down cover-fire while the others tried to set the explosive charge. One of their shots ricocheted and hit Sam's leg. Jerry let go with cover-fire as Steve quickly whipped out a bandage and stopped the bleeding—luckily, it wasn't an arterial wound.

Steve addressed the interface in his jacket pocket, "I hope someone's here and listening. Get our people near the quarters seal to move back immediately and prepare for an explosion. Have them put on their masks. It'll blow any second now! And hey, Sam's been hit! I've stabilized the wound, but we'll need to get him to Doc Smithson soon."

A female voice came from the interface, "This is Judy, Steve. Gotcha—on all counts."

Steve directed Jerry to a position behind the remaining concrete work of the nearest missile cradle. As Jerry crawled toward it, Steve opened fire on the four with his assault rifle. Then Jerry applied cover-fire, while Steve dragged Sam to Jerry's position. Steve was taking aim on the man leaning over the explosives, when the men bolted for the cover of the tunnel across the cavern.

Steve yelled, "Cover your ears!" There was a thunderous explosion at the quarters seal. When the smoke cleared, they could see the seal had been breached. The heavy steel doors had been blown out of their tracks and lay on the floor.

The men in the tunnel charged toward the breached seal with their weapons blazing. But they hadn't counted on Roxy. From a position well down the dark corridor to their quarters, she took aim with the RPG launcher and pulled the trigger. The rocket blazed through the quarters seal and exploded in the midst of the advancing assailants. She quickly loaded a second grenade and fired at the retreating survivors. After the second grenade exploded, there was no one left to retreat.

Outside, Dan had felt the first explosion and the grenades. He was checking on Jessica, she was coming around. Wally was nearby. Terra was there too, licking Jessica's face. The child had a nasty bump on the back of her head, which she rubbed as she looked up at her father. "Hi, Daddy. My head hurts."

"Hi, Sweet Pea. I'm sorry." Dan quickly scoped out the immediate area and asked, "Can you get to your feet, honey? I need to get you to a safer spot."

"I think so." Jessica first got to her knees and then, haltingly, stood up.

"That's great, honey. Take Terra with you and go down to the base of the incline near the stream, and around the corner. Keep quiet and stay low, okay?"

"Sure, Daddy."

"Wally will stay with you."

Wally gave Dan a casual salute and followed Jessica.

Three of the barricaders' trucks had made it behind the shield wall surrounding the silo building. A fourth was just inside the compound, a burning wreck. Dan had opened the heavy door to the silo building for the survivors, and they now had the use of the weaponry commandeered from Agent Bailey's van three days earlier.

Dan had Senator Brighton raise the stacks and turn on the ventilators, in reverse, to evacuate the poison gas pooling in the warren.

Jerry Sterling had gotten Sam safely out of the silo and into the infirmary. Steve was taunting the last surviving raider underground. The man was up on the lower elevator landing.

Steve yelled to him and, with a flashlight, directed his attention to the remains of his comrades lying on the silo floor. With that, the man dropped his weapon to the floor below.

When Jerry returned, Steve was waiting outside the quarters seal in Roxy's van, with the RPG. He had retrieved the man from the elevator landing and had him cuffed to the plumbing near the engineering cavern door.

When they'd made it up to the tunnel doors, Steve hopped out and opened them wide, to improve draft for the ventilators. Above them, up the ramp to the compound, small arms fire was nearly continuous. Once they had the van out onto the platform, they aired it out and removed their masks.

Finally, Jerry made his way down to the stream for Jessica. He found Terra sprawled across the girl, protecting her from the violence around them.

"Hi, Punkin."

"Hi, Jerry."

"Are you okay?"

"The guns were scaring me. I tried to tell Terra that Wally was here with us and that everything would be okay, but she insisted on protecting me herself."

The collie growled and snapped at Jerry as he reached for Jessica. "Whoa, girl! It's me, Jerry." Terra sniffed his hand and decided he was okay. She dropped her guard, wagged her tail, and got up.

Jerry said, "I guess they scared Terra too."

He lifted Jessica and carried her back up the incline, where he laid her down on some soft things in the back of the van. The collie piled in after her. "I want you and Terra to stay here, honey. Okay?"

"Sure, Jerry, I like it better in here."

"Jerry. Steve," said Dan from the interface in Steve's pocket. "Thanks, fellas. Our friends from the barricade have the remainder of these boys pinned down. They haven't been able to make it back to their choppers."

"Where are they?" asked Jerry.

"North of us, at the edge of the clearing."

Still armed, Jerry and Steve cautiously scaled the inclined drive, passed around the silo dome, and tried to see what was going on. They hunkered down and looked northward. Their remaining adversaries were pinned down at the edge of the clearing.

They watched as four desperate survivors made a run for the big, dark mass sitting motionless nearby. Three of the men made it through the rifle fire and disappeared inside the black hulk. The chopper's engine turned over and the large rotor began to spin. Bullets from the compound struck the craft's skin and glassy eyes. In a few moments, the main rotor had gained sufficient speed to lift the craft—it slowly took to the air.

Steve had the impulse to run after the RPGs in the van, but decided against it. He'd seen enough death and had done enough killing to last him a lifetime.

When the craft had reached sufficient altitude to clear the encircling trees it turned northward, dipped its nose, and started to accelerate. Just then, a ribbon of fire reached out from a position near the north end of the silo dome, and struck the craft. The chopper exploded in a thunderous fireball. Burning wreckage flew in all directions. Jerry and Steve ducked for cover.

Chapter 22

When it was over, they had one slightly-used helicopter, a second in a million pieces, twenty-one hostile's bodies, and four prisoners (three wounded, and one unscathed). The eighteen survivors of those who'd come down from the barricade, had lost six of their number, including four who had died in the truck hit by an RPG, another four had been wounded. And there was Sam's leg. And they'd also lost Pete. Dr. Smithson and Roxy, even with Sarah and Marsha's help, had had their hands full.

Steve and Jerry took the wounded barricaders, and the worst off of the raiders, to a hospital in Santa Fe and called the FBI. The agents showed up after midnight and stayed on the scene all night and into the morning. The Bureau had jurisdiction; a U.S. Senator had been the subject of an attempted assassination.

When it became obvious the chopper's ownership might be impossible to trace, its serial numbers had been removed, the agents decided that the Duttons might be seen to have certain rights to it, in compensation for damages. The FBI took all weaponry and ammunition from the craft, in addition to what Steve left them from the raid. Steve had stashed a portion of the raiders' arms and ammunition for later contingencies.

When all was said and done, the remaining wounded raiders departed for the hospital in FBI custody, while the county medical examiner hauled off the dead in a refrigerated truck. The lone, uninjured assailant, though handcuffed, was roughly shoved into one of the Bureau cars.

The Special Agent in Charge had had a lengthy talk with Senator Brighton about the events since President Forester's death.

Before the Bureau's arrival, Dan had questioned the survivors. As he expected, they had been experienced mercenaries—ex-commandos and the like, several British, two South African, six from Central America. Most were American citizens, with the majority being expats in the country only for this operation. Their commander, a French colonel, had survived with a head wound. Their original staging point had been in a mountainous area south of the border.

When questioned about his employer, Col. LaForte convincingly claimed to have been given orders and payment via a complicated third-party route. He had no idea which particular vested interest had hired him, though they'd been well compensated. They had each been paid $200,000 in advance (much more for the colonel) with more to come when their work was successfully completed. It had been worth millions to someone to have Dutton's associates relegated to the ranks of the disembodied. Dan made an educated guess as to who might profit most from seeing his work slowed or stopped.

The most puzzling aspect of the raid had been its timing. How had they known that Jessica had left the tunnel door open? Dan had gotten part of the answer when Steve found one of the scratchpad interfaces in the remaining helicopter.

The device had been manned for the purposes of the raid by a hapless young father, Josh Warner. Josh had been murdered and then forced to do their bidding, under the threat that his wife and children would be next. Warner had spied on Dutton's compound and reported the first opportunity to the raiders, who'd been waiting with their helicopters in the mountains nearby. Dan saw it as the saddest possible use of his efforts. He vowed to find Warner's family and bring them to safety.

Thursday afternoon, everyone, including Sam on crutches, met in the big living room. Dan said, "I believe we can go about our business now without worrying about being attacked. We're going to stop living like we're in a war zone. And for a little added peace of mind, I'm having Doppler radar installed to give us warning if even a hostile bumble bee comes our way, and a panic system on the ventilation and door closures."

"Unless you need me here, Dan," said Senator Brighton, "I think we'd better be getting back to Washington."

Ted Forester added, "If, as you say, there are no hostiles out there now, we really do need to be getting on with it. I've got work to do"

"You're right," replied Dan. "After all, travel time isn't a problem for folks in our condition, Ted. We can confer at a moment's notice—quicker than calling me in from the next room."

"It's occurred to me, Dan," said Forester, "that I'm going to need some especially close support from the living—for a while at least. I haven't asked, but I thought Roxy and Sam might be interested in helping me out, at least early on. I know Roxy isn't one to let people walk all over her. That's an essential quality in the Capitol."

By the look on her face, it was obvious Roxy had no idea the President had considered making such an offer. "I...I don't know what to say, Sir. Mr. President. I'd be honored to help you, if Dan doesn't mind. But my first allegiance will always be to Dan and his work."

"I don't mind, Roxy," said Dan. "There are going to be some interesting times ahead in Washington. It's a great opportunity. I think you should take it."

Roxy smiled that beaming smile of hers. "What do you think, Sam?"

"I agree. It sounds like a great opportunity. I'd like to help out too."

"I thought so." To President Forester, Roxy said, "I'll be ready whenever you are, Sir."

"Thank you, Roxy," said Forester. We'll go as soon as Senator Brighton makes his travel arrangements. I want you to know that I understand your allegiance to Dan. I feel the same. It's not a problem. In the meantime, maybe the girls would like to help you acquire a wardrobe for the Capitol. I don't think they're quite ready for your tattered blue jeans. You're going to be very much out in the open from now on. There's no doubt the cameras will be much happier with your pretty face than they ever were with my old, battle-worn puss."

"Sam," said Dan, "if you're going to be here a bit longer, I'd like you to help me assess what we need to do to get this place back in working order again."

Sam nodded and said, "I'd be glad to, sir."

The next day, Dan located Josh Warner's family and made plans to care for them.

Two weeks later, Marsha and Jerry were married and immediately departed for their honeymoon in northern Italy. Never known to do anything halfway, the Italians treated them like royalty.

Chapter 23

Two months later, Constitutional Amendment XXVIII was ratified by all fifty states. It guaranteed that all constitutional rights and protections would be preserved after death. The only qualification was proof of identity, thus necessitating the establishment of the Federal Late Center and its Special Courts and Advocates. The scratchpad interface would prove itself a strong tool in establishing identity. In addition, the amendment permitted Ted Forester to run for his old job.

Morgan Baills' impeachment by the House was followed by his suicide on the evening of the first day of his trial before the Senate.

Ted Forester was re-elected President by a landslide vote in a special election held in early December.

The Duttons soon moved back to their home in Albuquerque, where Jessica could live something more like a normal childhood. Dan resumed writing and inventing. Ned, their little mechanical Garden Guardian, had kept their yard pest and weed-free, and soon took to sleeping beside Terra at night, while he recharged.

Marsha Sterling waited for her producer's signal. She was seated behind a desk that night (she normally would have been standing for the broadcast). Marsha was into the eighth month of her pregnancy and had been on her feet much of the day.

Barney's camera was rolling. She was on.

"Hello, I'm Marsha Sterling and welcome to *New World Magazine*. It's been exactly two years since the world learned the truth about life and death. Since then we've seen many changes. Let's see what's happened during the past week.

"Yesterday, there was a big first birthday party and barbecue for Roxy and Sam Redhawk's son, Daniel. Roxy had taken the day off from her Washington job as

President Forester's spokesperson and, for that matter, so had her boss and most of his cabinet." Footage of the festivities played as Marsha narrated.

"The late Alvin Sheets and codefendant Jeremy Wills (Wills seen here being escorted from the federal courthouse in handcuffs) gave long-awaited testimony today against renowned psychiatrist Leonard Palkin, founder of Boston's Palkin Institute. Palkin has been charged as a primary conspirator in the crash of *Air Force One*, almost two years ago, and the murder of the staff and crew traveling with President Forester and his wife, Linda.

"The two testified that Palkin and his associates had funneled funds through Sheets' organization, for the purpose of financing the assassination effort by a group of conspirators that included the then-Vice President, Morgan Baills.

"Federal prosecutors claim that Palkin's funds came from a Swiss account belonging to a consortium with an address in Innsbruck, Austria.

"In Florence, a beloved Renaissance master, deceased since the early sixteenth century, is again at work painting for the first time in nearly five hundred years. He is withholding his identity so that the world might know him by his work alone." The screen filled with the image of a painting in the works. Holding the brush, applying paint to the canvas, is a mechanical hand reaching from off-camera. "The brush is held by a mechanical hand, but the master's style, technique, and skill are unmistakable."

"And now, we have a very special treat. Daniel Dutton is here with us tonight. It's been a while, Daniel. Thank you for accepting our invitation."

"It's my pleasure, Marsha." Dutton's voice was coming from an adjacent foxtail device. Daniel himself was seated nearby. "Glad to be with you."

"It's quite a different world we live in today from what it was two years ago. What have you been up to?"

"Well, as you might be aware, I've gotten back to writing. Two new novels. But my real passion these days has been a new line of investigation—something that has yielded yet another unique application out of existing technologies."

"And what is that? I had no idea you were up to anything but writing."

"It's a camera."

"A camera? What sort of camera?"

"Well, to get right to the point, it's a digital camera designed to record mental images."

"A what? It records mental pictures? Like thoughts and memories?"

"Uh-huh, though at this point, it's limited to still photography. I'm working on a video version."

"Honestly, Daniel, I don't know if I can wrap my wits around what that means. What will come of this new technology of yours?"

"Well. Let's just think about it. Aside from what the foxtail and related technologies have brought us in understanding our own true nature, the sciences themselves have remained pretty much unchanged. Our knowledge of the universe and even our grasp of history, particularly archaeology and prehistory, remain pretty much what they were preceding these innovations."

Marsha shook her head and asked, "What do history and archaeology have to do with your camera?"

"Everything! As it turns out, this tool opens up new vistas of experience—the past, even the distant past."

"I don't think I follow you, Dan. The past? Distant past?"

"Well, if we can record an individual's memories, we have a tool for investigating recent events. Like what they've witnessed. If they've been a witness to a crime, we have a recording of the event available to the prosecution in courts of law. Or, if they've witnessed some natural calamity, like the Russian meteor-strike, we have recordings available in great resolution—from witnesses, from victims."

"I see what you mean," said Marsha. "This could add perspective to our view of...of everything."

"This," said Dan, "is an entirely new kettle of fish. It's the subjective tool that will augment the technologies of objective science and put all of existence in an entirely new light. It's a powerful tool for the humanities, history, the natural sciences. The possibilities are mind-boggling."

"You *have* been busy!" stated Marsha.

"Yes. And then, of course, there are the little ones."

"The little ones?"

"Those who've benefited from the interface technology and have come back."

"Come back?"

"We've seen it statistically, in just two years. Many late individuals just disappear. They decide to move on—to try it again, to perhaps pick up where they'd left off. Or maybe with an aim to making better life choices."

"You've seen this statistically?"

"Absolutely. A significant percentage hang around a while and eventually say, "I'm going back!" And they do. They disappear from the rolls of the re-enfranchised and are gone. Gone until they show up again as little ones, among the living. Some even return to be born again into the same families, to be with those they've loved and missed."

"Oh, my God!" said Marsha. Out of the camera's field of view (behind the desk) she patted her distended belly, wondering what might be ahead for her little family.

"We're seeing it now," said Daniel, "But this is not new in human experience. The German newborn, speaking within hours of birth. The inconsolable young girl, just beginning to talk, worried sick about the husband and children she'd abruptly left behind at her death. The newly-deceased who so often show up to say good-bye. And all of it before we had the interface. These things happened, these occurrences were real and often on the record. Sure, at the time they were negated by the media, by those out to limit man to a finite span of years—to being just dust in the wind.

"Today it is unarguable fact. Soon, we of planet Earth, will fully grasp how much we are responsible for our own futures. How we create the world we leave behind at our death. So, let's do our utmost to make it a world we would want to be born into. 'Where,' as President Forester has expressed it, 'We have left behind the history of greed and violence our mortal view had given us.'"

"I could go on, Marsha, but what I want to do now is share a few things I've become aware of—having been in my current state long enough to pay attention to what I've had available to me all along."

"What things?" asked Marsha.

"Several things for which I now have objective proof—realities I can share in high-resolution, un-retouched photography. It's not just my say so.

"While we've been talking, Marsha—my wife, Sarah, has provided your production crew with three high-resolution photographs. She's given them three still images for you to share with your audience. These are images from my own personal history. Images where I'm a witness and an observer. Mental images I've recorded with this new device."

Marsha asked, "Are you serious, Daniel? I...my producer is nodding her head." She pressed a finger to her earphone. "I guess we're...I guess we're ready. Will you please give us some sort of narration, Daniel?"

"I will. Please go ahead and show the first image."

The first image appeared on a large screen beside Marsha. "Oh, my Lord, Daniel. Is...is this what it appears to be?"

"Sadly, yes. This is as it appears. An image of a Roman mass crucifixion of Christians along the Appian Way, occurring in the years following the Crucifixion of Christ."

"It's...it's so monstrous."

There were exclamations from the production crew, themselves overtaken with the impact of the image.

Daniel said, "Okay, let's go to the second image."

A new image appeared. Marsha said, "Those are...those are The Pyramids. And The Great Pyramid! And they...one is under construction."

"Yes," explained Daniel, "This image answers an age-old question. How were the huge stones—here being transported up to the level of the Plateau of Giza—how were they transported from the Nile to the level of the construction site? This site was old in Hellenistic times. Today, it's the last surviving wonder of the *Seven Wonders of the Ancient World.*"

"I...oh, my gosh! It's so simple!" exclaimed Marsha. "Why hasn't anyone thought of this possibility before now?"

"They haven't spoken with someone who was there."

"This is so mind-boggling! It's...it's wonderful!"

The third and final image at first baffled Marsha.

Dan didn't supply any narration. He left it up to her to interpret. It was an image of a huge arching interior space, with what must have been many hundreds of travelers making their way around what appeared to be a travel terminal. Above it all was a beautiful huge representation of the Milky Way Galaxy, in full relief on the far wall. It hung above a busy throng moving away from and toward the viewer along broad moving walkways that disappeared into the distance beneath it.

"Oh my Lord, Daniel! Is this what it appears to be?"

"What is that, Marsha?"

"I don't know how else to interpret it, even their clothing. It looks...it looks for all the world like...like a space terminal!"

The doorbell rang.

Jessica answered the front door and found a four-year-old boy with curly blonde hair and a familiar smile. He was seated on a shiny red tricycle. She recognized him instantly.

"Hi!" said Jessica."

He winked a familiar wink and said, "Hi, Jessy. Wow! You've grown up to be quite the big girl. Can't say the same for myself." He looked down at his own little body, then back to Jessica. "Oh, well...gotta start somewhere."

"It's been a long time," said Jessica. "Way too long. I've missed you!"

"I've missed you too, Jessy."

"I like your trike."

"Thanks." The little guy looked down at his shiny tricycle. "I like it too. It was my birthday present—four-years-old."

Terra rushed out the door and nuzzled the boy without hesitation, lifting his hand with her muzzle, hoping to be petted. The boy rubbed Terra's back in her favorite spot. The children smiled and giggled. The collie recognized him too.

"Wow! Has it been that long?"

"Yep. I start school next week on account of my birthday's in December."

Jessica replied, "That's cool. I didn't start until I was five."

He smiled that familiar smile again and said, "Anyway, I just wanted to stop by and say hi! Is your dad home?"

"Yeah, he's here. Let me call him."

Jessica disappeared into the house. She could be heard yelling, "Daddy, there's someone at the door for you!"

Jessica returned with a foxtail phone in her hand.

From inside, her father said, "Who is it? I'm busy!"

She smiled a knowing smile, looked at their grinning long-lost visitor, and yelled her reply, "It's...it's Jason, Daddy."

Jessica grinned, leaned over and whispered in Jason's ear, "This is gonna be good!"

The End

Author's Note

While this story is fiction, the devices it depicts are within our reach using existing technologies.

The incident involving the stereo, in the opening sequence, actually happened. It occurred exactly as depicted, during the wee hours of the same night I had completed the first draft of this work, which included the author's note.

The flower being drawn on the phone screen also actually took place. The image used in this work's jacket art is an un-retouched copy of that original.

Thank you, Mel, for your flower.

My sincere thanks to Mary, Autumn, Emmy, Cindy, Bill, Melissa, and Rachael for their encouragement and support.

Special thanks to my friend,
Charles A. Madison, for offering the definitive encouragement.

www.ingramcontent.com/pod-product-compliance
Lightning Source LLC
Chambersburg PA
CBHW020247150626
46552CB00020B/644